Dilemmas:

Aces and

Eights

Diane Hilyard Brown

Prologue

Life is much like a game of poker. During the course of a game you can be dealt an equal share of good hands and bad hands. You can leave the table with the same amount of money you sat down with, depart with empty pockets, or exit with pockets full. On rare occasion, you can play the hand you're dealt. More often than not you must throw away the bad cards and draw to make a better hand. And then there are the unfortunate instances when you are forced to fold, giving up all claims to the pot, and wait for the next hand, hoping it will be better.

In the game of love, Delilah Leigh Beauregard was always dealt aces and eights, more commonly known as dead man's hand; five husbands, five dead man's hands.

But to understand the source of Delilah's plight, one must go back in time to the year 1819. In the small village of Lizella, Georgia, twelve miles west of Macon, lived a rich and powerful man named Morris Bogart; a boisterously cruel, yet devilishly charming man, devoid of scruples or the slightest measure of compassion. In addition to pulling the strings of the townsfolk like a master puppeteer, he often made sport of philandering with young virgins, in addition to the consenting wives of the men whose lives he so readily manipulated.

In contrast, there also lived a loving, devoted family man named Maurice Beauregard. Through honest, hard work and a knack for evading the clutches of Morris, Maurice had amassed a sizeable fortune and property half way between Lizella and Macon, where a grand mansion had been constructed for his wife and three sons.

In the spring of 1819 a blossoming, virtuous beauty named Helena Price fell victim to the charms of Morris Bogart. As was his custom, he lured the innocent girl into his bed with promises of marriage, and then promptly abandoned her when she was with child.

Outraged at the betrayal, Helena sought unconventional retribution by means of Zylphia;

an old hag who lived deep in the woods just a few miles north of town.

On rare occasions Zylphia would appear in the village, some would say out of thin air. Though children and strangers were warned not to meet her gaze, one could not help but stare at the creature with long, wiry, gray hair, and filthy, colorless clothes that draped in shreds over folds of withered skin.

"She practices black magic," the townsfolk would say. "How else could she live this long?" "She was old when my grandmother was a girl." "There's just something unnatural about her."

Notwithstanding cautions, Helena forged through two miles of thick underbrush until she came upon Zylphia's dilapidated shack. Her desire for revenge overpowering her fear, she knocked on the door.

"Come in, Helena," Zylphia growled.

After a moment's hesitation in which Helena reconsidered her choice, she pushed the door open.

"It is Helena, is it not?" Zylphia asked as Helena stepped into the dimly lit room.

"Yes, ma'am," Helena replied, her voice quivering with anxiety.

The old hag, who was nearly deaf, and just as blind, stepped closer to Helena. Overcome by a foul stench, Helena retreated slightly, only to stumble over several mangy cats pacing at her feet.

"You come in pursuit of revenge," Zylphia stated.

"Yes, ma'am," Helena said.

Zylphia cupped her hand to her ear, and squinted. "Ay!" she bellowed.

"Yes, ma'am," Helena repeated a little louder. "My virtue has been compromised by Morris Bogart."

"Ah," Zylphia groaned as she nodded. "And what would you have done?"

"It is my wish, my request that the first born male of the Bogart family meet with misfortune for eternity. Or, that is to say, at the very least until the Bogart family bestows sufficient recompense in the form of marriage to a Price. However, I am willing to accept the totality of their property as a compromise," Helena replied.

"I see," Zylphia said, looking the girl up and down. "That will require a very complex curse. How do you intend to compensate me?"

"I have very little," Helena said disappointedly.

"Your child, perhaps?" Zylphia inquired.

Helena paused to give thought to the proposition. Her reputation was ruined. Her chances of making a good marriage with a respectable man were nonexistent, and she had no means to support herself and a child. What little concern she harbored for the welfare of the child was quickly consumed by her selfish needs.

"Very well," she said. "You may have the child."

Zylphia placed a black cauldron on the grate above the embers in the fireplace, and set about pouring the contents of various vials into the cauldron. Twice, during this process, Helena attempted to depart, and twice she was told she must stay.

As the concoction began to boil, Zylphia began searching the floor."Here kitty," she called. Within seconds a cat darted from beneath the table, and the old woman snatched it in her hands.

"The whisker of a male cat," she screamed as she plucked a whisker from the terrified feline, and dropped it into the cauldron.

"That cat is a female!" Helena exclaimed.

"Ay!" Zylphia questioned.

Helena raised the tail of the squirming cat, and pointed.

"Oh, well," Zylphia said with a wince and a shrug. "First born male, first born female, doesn't really matter, does it?"

Helena shook her head and rolled her eyes in disgust.

Acid green smoke began spiraling from the cauldron. Zylphia quickly took a hand full of salt from a tin container, and slowly added it to the mixture as she recited the incantation: "Toil and trouble, love most hard, for descendants of Maurice Beauregard."

"No, you crazy old woman!" Helena shouted. "Not Maurice Beauregard. Morris Bogart!"

The old woman's eyes went wide. "Well, that can't be good," she said.

"Fix it!" Helena shouted.

But before Zylphia could correct her mistake, she was overcome by the fumes of the toxic brew, and fell to the floor clutching her chest. Within seconds the old woman had expired.

Without a care one for the dearly departed, Helena hastened from the scene enraged that her revenge would be exacted on the wrong party, and vowing she would never speak of the episode.

And so, she kept her secret; that is until she lay on her deathbed, at which point she conveyed the story to the doctor tending her. Her confession fell on suspicious ears, however, as she had also intimated that she was an Egyptian queen owing to the fact that she had been the wife of Cleopatra's son, Herman.

In the mean time, Maurice Beauregard's first-born granddaughter, Malinda, began experiencing the effects of the malediction. One hundred, thirty years, and four generations later, Delilah joined the ranks of cursed, first-born, female Beauregards.

Chapter 1

Beauregard Bequest

In her youth Delilah Leigh Beauregard was said to have been the incarnation of heaven's most beautiful angels; bright sea-blue eyes, and hair that flowed like black satin ribbons in perfect ringlets against her flawless alabaster skin.

As Delilah grew older, her cherubic features became more refined and striking. The only child of Macon, Georgia's Buford and Hannah Beauregard might have been the complete Southern-belle package, had it not been for the misfortune that accompanied her like a mischievous shadow.

Despite the constant companionship of calamity, Delilah rarely lost her sense of humor or quick wit, often times joking about, as opposed to questioning, her propensity for bad luck. This lent an endearing quality to the raven haired beauty.

Buford was an affluent man who owned one of the oldest antebellum homes in Georgia. The palatial, two-story, Greek revival structure sat in the center of a substantial parcel of land that had been owned by the Beauregard family for nearly two centuries. Buford himself was no stranger to substance, standing 6 feet, 4 inches tall, and weighing in at a hefty 350 pounds.

Delilah had genetically inherited her mother's good looks, but the similarities ended there. Hannah was considerably petite while Delilah was 5 feet, 8 inches tall and curvy. Hannah was selfishly mindful of appearances and social graces. Delilah was altruistic and natural. In short, Hannah was a pretentious snob, Delilah was not.

Through the years, Hannah had over compensated for Delilah's unfortunate mishaps by forcing her child to endure the tedium of social climbing. All the while her daughter's nature rebelled. Inevitably this tug of war caused a perceptible tension between the two women; a stark contrast to the relationship between father and daughter. Buford was putty in Delilah's hands.

"I'm getting you a car for your birthday, Princess," Buford proclaimed in his deep southern drawl, just days before Delilah's sixteenth birthday. "Whatever you want."

"Oh, thank you, Big Daddy," Delilah sang with excitement as she threw her arms around his massive neck. "But with my luck, I probably need to drive an army tank. You can't get me one of those, can you?"

Buford laughed heartily with his daughter, and embraced her tightly.

Hannah, on the other hand, rolled her eyes, and sighed. "For cryin' out loud, Delilah!" she snapped. "You're a Beauregard. You should be drivin' Cadillac's."

"You do know, Mother," Delilah said sardonically, "all the Cadillac's in the world, all the beauty pageants, finishing schools, debutante balls, country club teas, manicures, pedicures and designer clothing won't magically lift the Beauregard curse from me, or transform me into the social icon you want me to be."

"You have a duty to the Beauregard name, and this community?" Hannah lectured. "And once again, there is no such thing as the

Beauregard curse! You're getting a Cadillac! That's final!" she screeched.

Two years, and three new Cadillac's later, Delilah was sent away to college in a super-sized SUV she'd named Bertha, after Buford's failed attempt to procure her a "tank on wheels" from his long-time friend, Lieutenant Colonel Wapford.

While at college, Delilah was pursued by a multitude of suitors, and eventually fell in love with James Jasper Hamilton, IV. He was funny and kind, which suited Delilah, and handsome and rich, which suited Hannah.

One week after receiving her degree in Interior Design, four hundred and fifty two guests were assembled in St. Peter's Cathedral, the largest church in Macon, awaiting the social event of the decade; Delilah's ceremonial walk down the aisle. One of the guests was Buford's twin sister, Nettie Mae.

By all accounts, Nettie Mae was the black sheep of the family, and Delilah's favorite relative. A large woman both literally and figuratively, who was considered by most to be nuttier than squirrel poo, and often referred to as the Norma

Desmond of the Beauregard clan. Though, in all fairness, Nettie never killed anyone she shot.

Nettie Mae owned a ranch in Oklahoma. It was always rumored that she had acquired the property in a high stakes game of poker, and then promptly changed the name to The Royal Flush Ranch. At Hannah's insistence, Nettie Mae's questionable business transactions, and life in general, were taboo topics for discussion.

As a child, Delilah spent many a summer with her aunt in Oklahoma where she was allowed to ride horses, make mud pies, sleep out under the stars, and just be a kid. She was also exposed to a side of Nettie that very few others had ever seen; the softer, more compassionate side. And Nettie always seemed to understand Delilah better than anyone else.

"Aunt Nettie?" the ten year old Delilah began one hot summer afternoon, as she swung in a tire that dangled from the branch of a tall sycamore tree. "Why do you suppose Mother gets so upset with me when things go wrong? I mean, it's not like I deliberately set out to make the crazy things happen."

14

Nettie smiled, as she lay on an old quilt spread out under the tree. True to form the child had not questioned why the "crazy things" always happened to her. She had accepted it, but she couldn't understand why her mother had not.

"Well, I just don't think you're meant to be a socialite, and the more your mother tries to change your nature the more nature fights back," Nettie said, still smiling. "Your mother has never been very good with resistance, and any way that's not her way, is resistance. I think she means well, child. It's just that her idea of what's best for you may not actually be what's best for you. And whatever you do, don't tell her I said that."

"You don't have to worry about that," Delilah said with a chuckle.

Eleven years later, the two sat in a corner of the bride's room off the Church's foyer. Lightning flashed, thunder roared and rain poured beyond the walls of the massive structure.

Nettie whispered softly, "Do you love this man?"

"Very much," Delilah replied with a broad smile and a twinkle in her eyes.

"You're not marrying him to appease the queen, are you?" Nettie said with a jerk of her head in Hannah's direction.

Delilah laughed. "No."

"Of course it would storm on your wedding day, Delilah," Hannah sneered, making her way toward the two in the corner. "And for the love of Pete, stand up, child. You're going to wrinkle your dress."

A man knocked on the door and announced to the occupants that it was time. Just as the wedding march sounded, so did the tornado sirens. Thirty minutes later, the sardine packed crowd immerged from the church basement to a windowless and roofless sanctuary.

Fast forward twenty years. Nettie Mae had passed away unexpectedly. She had been buried, and the Beauregard family, all clad in black, was gathered in the living room of Nettie's hundred-year old, two-story farm house, waiting for the reading of her will. The rustic setting halfway between Cushing and Stroud, Oklahoma, was a far cry from the family's opulent origins in Macon, Georgia.

The house sat on top of a high hill, about a quarter mile off the road, facing east. Once off the road, the gravel drive curved to the right, and then back to the left, around the dam side of a pond. At midpoint of the dam, a wooden bridge crossed a creek which allowed for overflow from the pond. A number of mature oak, elm, pecan and sycamore trees were randomly scattered the distance of the drive, opposite the pond. After passing the dam, the drive began its steep climb, and slight curve back to the right to the top of the hill, where the house sat on the north side of the drive. A two-car garage apartment, which had recently been built, was positioned at an angle about forty feet behind the house.

Once at the top of the hill, the drive curved right, into the parking area. To the left, a rutted, gravel lane passed a fenced enclosure, the well house, and a propane tank. Further down the lane about a hundred yards sat the old, wooden barn, in desperate need of paint, and the corral. Beyond the barn, the drive continued southwest a few hundred yards to a mobile home parked in a pecan grove. The mobile home had always been occupied by the ranch foreman.

"Buford, what are we going to do with all this junk?" Hannah said with a scowl as she motioned around the living room. "I suppose we could hire an auctioneer to dispose of it."

"Mother!" Delilah exclaimed in horror. "There are a good number of valuable antiques here. Not to mention several items of great sentimental value; at least to me."

"It's just a bunch of old stuff, Delilah," Hannah argued.

Nettie Mae's attorney pulled a document from his briefcase, cleared his throat while straightening his red bowtie, and began reading. "I, Nettie Mae Beauregard, being of sound mind and body,"

Half the people in the room shook their heads, while the other half rolled their eyes. Delilah just hung her head. The loss of her aunt had taken a toll on her. She worried that her precious aunt's treasures would be treated with contemptuous indifference, much like Nettie Mae had been treated the better part of her adult life. The attorney droned on and on for what seemed like an eternity.

"And to my darling niece, Delilah Leigh Beauregard Hamilton Fisher Smith Conner Smith, I bequeath all remaining property and personal effects."

Delilah's head rose slowly, unsure of what she'd just heard. Her eyes locked on the attorney's eyes. He was smiling.

"What?" eight voices exclaimed in long, southern-drawl unison.

"There is a stipulation, however," the attorney interjected nervously. "The property, whole or in part, cannot be liquidated for a period of five years."

Hannah shot up from the sofa. "Well, clearly the woman was deranged!" she shrieked as she spun like a top to confront Buford. "I swear, Buford, she did this just to irritate me. As if leaving me that ridiculous, gaudy brooch of hers wasn't irritation enough. She knew I abhorred that hideous piece of junk. And she knew I'd object to Delilah owning this run down piece of property."

"I wonder, Hannah," Uncle Gene said calmly and politely. "Has it ever occurred to you that not everything in this world is about *you?*" The much younger brother of the Beauregard twins was the only family member capable of putting Hannah in her place without first sending her into spastic fits of hysteria; a condition generally managed by controlled pharmaceuticals.

Delilah held back the urge to laugh at her uncle's comment. She recalled her youthful summers spent with her favorite aunt, playing dress-up with the brooch in question, as well as numerous other big, chunky pieces of jewelry her mother detested. Nettie's Irish setter, Rose, had patiently allowed Delilah to drape beads and bobbles from nose-tip to tail's end. Delilah chuckled under her breath at the thought.

Mr. Thomas, the attorney, cleared his throat again, and Delilah returned to the issue at hand. "Am I to understand, Mrs. Beauregard, you do *not* wish to accept the gift Nettie Mae has left you?"

"I certainly do not!" Hannah exclaimed crassly. "And Delilah will be declining her gift as well."

Before Delilah could object to, or confirm her mother's proclamation, a fidgeting Mr. Thomas continued with his inquiry. "Does anyone else wish to decline that which has been bequeathed to them?"

Gene's wife, Jean, responded first, indicating that the collection of children's books left to her might be nice to have for her grandchildren. Their son, Sonny, declined the horse left to him, stating he had "nowhere to put the poor beast," and their youngest daughter, Sammie, pleasantly and graciously accepted the twenty-inch strand of black pearls left to her.

All that remained was the oldest of Gene and Jean Beauregard's children, Abigail. She was a social-climbing, money-grabbing, insensitive, malicious witch who hovered so low on her Oreck even NORAD couldn't detect her. She smiled; a twisted, devious, calculating smile that always preceded a counter offensive or curse. "Thank you, but I have no use for that silly child's drawing left to me," she hissed.

"Very well," Mr. Thomas said with a quick nod and a calculating smile of his own. "These decisions are binding and cannot be retracted, redirected, or otherwise altered. Is that understood?"

Everyone nodded their acceptance of the terms as they signed the waivers handed to them by Mr. Thomas; everyone except Delilah.

"Hold on just a minute," Delilah said as she rose from her chair and sauntered over to Nettie's massive, antique, oak desk. "I haven't given you my answer. And if it's all the same to you, I'd like a little more time to consider the matter."

"Consider what?" Hannah questioned incredulously. "For heaven's sake, child, you are not moving to Oklahoma. That's final."

"Mother," Delilah countered as she grasped a dusty, worn pair of boots beside the desk. "This *child* reached adulthood over two decades ago. Contrary to what you believe, I am capable of directing my own life. As I see it, all I have in Georgia is you, Big Daddy, the graves of five husbands, and the reputation for being a black widow."

"Oh, nonsense," Hannah huffed. "No one thinks you had any connection to the deaths of those five men."

Delilah plopped down in the chair at the desk and began removing the high heels from her feet. She could tell from the astonished looks on the faces of her family that her mother's statement was not entirely true.

"Except that I was married to all of them," Delilah said with amused sarcasm. She slipped her feet into the boots and stood. "Perfect fit. Now, if you'll excuse me, I'm going to walk down to the barn. Mr. Thomas, would you be kind enough to escort me? And bring your briefcase . . . we have a few things to discuss."

Mr. Thomas was impressed with the curvaceous, raven-haired beauty. Not only had she inherited her aunt's property but she had also, it appeared, inherited her commanding presence. This in tandem with the woman's sweet, southern charm and manners made for a triple threat. He no longer wondered why Delilah had had five husbands.

Delilah grabbed her black, fringed shawl from the arm of the sofa, and swung it around her shoulders. Mr. Thomas gathered the documents and placed them in his briefcase. And then the attorney followed her out the back door.

"So . . . what's the catch?" Delilah inquired wryly as the two strolled down the rutted dirt lane to the barn. After a brief silence she pressed on. "Don't pretend you don't know what I'm talking about, Mr. Thomas. I happen to know that the center stone of that 'ridiculous, gaudy brooch' is a five carat, Russian-mined Alexandrite. Exceptionally rare, and I suspect worth tens of thousands of dollars."

"Eighty-two thousand, the last time it was appraised." Mr. Thomas offered with a grin.

"And," Delilah trudged on. "I also know that 'the poor beast' Sonny so flippantly disregarded is a very valuable stud horse. And, beneath that 'silly child's drawing' Abby has no use for, is a priceless Renoir. Why didn't you tell them?"

"I was instructed not to tell them, Delilah. They have behaved just as Nettie Mae predicted they would. And their narrow mindedness has cost them dearly. She knew them considerably better than they knew her. Even her brothers are unfamiliar with those particular details."

Pausing a moment to appreciate the late winter sunset, Delilah took in a long breath of cool, country air, and gave serious thought to the attorney's insights. She wondered what else he'd been instructed not to divulge. She remembered with great fondness one of Nettie's many "life lessons" during her hiatus on the ranch, after the death of her first husband.

"You know, Delilah," Aunt Nettie said. "It's always important not to take things at face value. So often people and things aren't what they appear to be. For instance," she continued making a dramatic gesture toward the simple, framed drawing on the wall. "What do you think of this lovely drawing Abigail sent me when she was five years old?"

"I like it. It reminds me that Abigail was innocent and fun at one time," Delilah replied.

"Now what do you think of it?" Nettie said as she magically pulled the drawing out of the frame, revealing something else behind it.

Delilah was stunned. "Aunt Nettie, is that,"

"Yes dear, it's a Renoir."

Mr. Thomas cleared his throat while Delilah shrugged herself back into the present.

"Well, be that as it may," Delilah said. "I don't know that it's fair to withhold that information from them. At least let me tell Aunt Jean what the books are worth. I'm sure she has no idea they're all first editions. Otherwise she'll allow those hellions she calls grandchildren to completely destroy them."

The three hellions in question were the by-product of Abigail, and had mercifully been left in Macon with their equally obnoxious and disruptive father.

Delilah shot a cutting glance toward Mr. Thomas. "Just out of curiosity . . . how much are they worth?"

He laughed. "About seventy-five thousand for the entire collection."

The two reached the barn. Delilah rested her arms on the top rung of the corral. She drew in another deep breath and then sighed. "You still haven't answered my original question, Sir. I know there's a catch. I mean, aside from the obvious five year thing, my owning this property won't be as simple as just owning this property."

Mr. Thomas hesitated a moment. Choosing his words carefully, he cleared his throat, and began. "Delilah, your experience with . . . adversity puts you at a marked advantage over the others."

"Adversity?" Delilah repeated with raucous laughter. "That's certainly a diplomatic way of saying bad luck."

Mr. Thomas smiled. "Your knowledge of this place, the business, and Nettie's possessions, make you the perfect candidate to inherit. And yes, you are correct, it won't be simple. Your aunt believed, as I do now, that certain family members, one in particular, would contest her will. The estate is facing some financial . . . delicacies, and operating a ranch can just be plain, hard work."

Delilah nodded, giving careful consideration to the attorney's second diplomatic reference; financial *delicacies*. "I want to go over the books. I assume you have a copy of the financial statement."

"I have all the documents concerning the ranch," he confirmed. "I'll leave them with you tonight. You can give me your decision in the morning.

"One more thing, Delilah," Mr. Thomas said cautiously. "You won't have to contend strictly with family members who want a piece of this pie. There are others who want to get their hands on this property as well."

Chapter 2

Gus and Pandora

Stroud, Oklahoma is the halfway point between Oklahoma City and Tulsa on Interstate 44. Among other boasts, it is a stop along the famed Route 66. It was here that the family had gone to eat, and lodge for the night. Delilah opted to stay at The Royal Flush Ranch, free from the influence of her meddlesome mother, and conniving cousin.

The better part of Delilah's night was spent pouring over financial statements, and legal documents. The ranch was far from making money hand over fist. The primary source of income had been the stud horse her cousin Sonny had been willed, but thankfully declined. Though she was the daughter of a wealthy man, Delilah's own finances were substantially less impressive, bordering on abysmal.

The legal issues, much to her relief, appeared to be considerably less disconcerting than the financial issues. Delilah had become well versed in law by way of her second husband, Ambrose Fisher, a powerful lawyer and aspiring politician.

It was no secret Ambrose had divorced his wife to pursue and marry the attractive, young, widowed Delilah, eighteen years his junior. On more than one occasion Ambrose was heard saying, "I traded a bee in my bonnet for a feather in my cap," which was ironic because on the day of his inauguration as Governor of Georgia, while addressing a crowd of thousands on the lawn of the capitol, Ambrose was stung by a bee, and died within an hour.

The small fortune Ambrose had amassed was divided amongst his four children, ex-wife, and countless creditors, leaving Delilah with nothing more than the personal effects acquired during their four year marriage, and the Interior Design business in Macon he'd purchased for her as a wedding gift.

With three hours sleep to her credit, Delilah stumbled out of Nettie's four poster bed, and set about opening the plantation shutters to a gray, overcast day.

She made her way downstairs, opening shutters along the way, until she reached the antiquated kitchen, only to discover that a gray and white goat had somehow entered the back door during the night, and totally wrecked the room.

The drain rack had been toppled to the floor, and its contents scattered. The plastic cups and food containers were shredded beyond recognition. Dish towels were scattered in pieces on the floor and counter top. All that remained of a sack of potatoes was the sack, which also lay in pieces on the floor.

Clothed only in her finest blue, silk night gown, Delilah wrestled the goat off the counter top, removed the rubber drain board from its mouth, and pushed the four legged creature to the back door where she was met by an aged man.

He was tall and thin, and his faded, worn overalls hung loosely on his body. His salt and pepper hair was cut short, and the weathered, brown skin of his face framed a warm, but toothless smile.

"I am tho thorry, Mith Beauregard," he said, taking hold of the goat and pulling it out the door. He turned his head to the side and spat a stream of tobacco juice off the porch. "I didn't get the gate locked good lath night. I'll juth put Pandora back in her pen."

"Who are you?" Delilah asked abruptly, crossing her arms in front of her.

"I'm Guth, the ranch hand," he replied.

Clearly frightening the poor man with her outburst of laughter, obviously brought on by sleep deprivation, Delilah composed herself. "Oh! Oh, of course. Gus. I saw you at the funeral."

"Well, I didn't want to intrude, or I'd have introduthed mythelf earlier," he said.

Delilah robed herself, while Gus returned the goat to her pen, and thirty minutes later, with the assistance of the ranch hand, all evidence of Pandora's rampage was erased from the kitchen. It was during the clean-up Delilah was reminded that Gus occupied the mobile home beyond the barn.

Gus exited the house after declining Delilah's breakfast invitation, and Delilah adjourned to the living room where she sat in peace and quiet with her cup of coffee at the large, oak desk. She made a few phone calls, and after considerable effort, removed additional bank records from the securely wedged lap drawer.

After reviewing the records, she took a quick shower, then shimmied into a pair of blue jeans, and shrugged on a pink argyle sweater. As she made her way downstairs, the family arrived and dysfunction resumed.

In no time at all, the family had scattered like cock-roaches, and were pillaging through the contents of the house. With Hannah's assistance, Aunt Jean was packing the children's books bequeathed to her. Abigail and Sammie were rifling through linens and quilts. Uncle Gene and Sonny had gone to the garage to inventory tools. And Delilah, taking advantage of their preoccupations, coerced Buford outside onto the large porch that wrapped around the northeast corner of the old farmhouse.

"Mr. Thomas will be here in a bit, Daddy," Delilah said in a hushed tone. She pulled her shawl tighter around her shoulders. "I guess you know what this means."

"Yes, darlin', I know what it means," he acknowledged softly.

"I hope you're okay with this?" Delilah said. "I talked to Dooby earlier. He's going to load all my personal things in a trailer and bring them here."

"Delilah, honey, I think this will be a good move for you. I think that putting some distance between your past and the present, between you and your mother, will allow you to see things differently. You've always loved this place. Why not live here? And by the way, I talked to Dooby just after you did."

"Well, Momma's not screaming so it's safe to assume you haven't told her yet," Delilah declared. Buford laughed. "I thought I'd let you tell her."

"Thanks, a lot!" Delilah said morosely.

Certainly Hannah had *some* inkling that her only daughter could *possibly* be moving far away from her influential reach, which, in theory would temper her tantrum when the decision was

34

announced. However, the Dooby factor, as Delilah and Buford knew too well, would be that ever-so-slight nudge required to push Hannah over that fine line of reason and sanity she so regularly walked.

In a moment of panicked contemplation, Delilah briefly considered putting her mother in the pen with Pandora before breaking the news to her. But that seemed far too excessive a punishment for the goat.

Dooby had been Delilah's best friend since the age of five. He was the only child of Vernell and Vonda Kelly. Vernell owned the bait and tackle shop on Dames Ferry Road outside of Macon, and Vonda was an extraordinarily talented accountant, as well as one the most gifted psychics in Georgia.

Vonda occupied a corner in the bait shop. So, local anglers could purchase their bait and tackle, drop off their 1040's, and for an extra ten dollars, she could tell them how lucky they'd be at catching fish.

Though the Kelly's were one of the most respected and well liked African-American families in Macon, they were nonetheless, African-American. Hannah, steadfastly clinging to old prejudices, failed to appreciate Dooby's sweet, brotherly love and dedication to Delilah's well being. On more than one occasion Dooby had come between Delilah and her fated mayhem, quite possibly saving her life.

When Dooby was young, Vonda would always say "Do be polite," and "Do be careful," or "Do be on your best behavior," and "Do be watchin' out for Miss Delilah." In Delilah's child mind, the boy's name was Dooby; a name the boy happily accepted as an alternative to the unacceptable variations of Vernell Hezekiah the fourth.

With the arrival of Mr. Thomas, the family gathered once more in the large living room of Nettie Mae's old farm house, and the announcement was made that it was now Delilah's old farm house.

Abigail seethed in silence, while Hannah uncharacteristically smiled and sang her happy approval. Delilah momentarily suspected her father had slipped Hannah an extra "nerve" pill at breakfast, but quickly dispelled the idea when she saw the look of utter shock mixed with something resembling fear on Buford's face.

Uncle Gene and Aunt Jean congratulated her, as did Sammie, while Sonny appeared to be bored with the whole thing.

"Well, I guess that's settled then," Hannah said with a slightly bitter edge and a forced smile. It was evident Hannah's grip on civility was loosening. "Is there someone to look after this place while you're putting your affairs in order back home?"

"I'm staying here, Mother," Delilah said with determination. She inhaled deeply and squared her shoulders. "Dooby's bringing my things here."

There was a foreboding silence as Hannah's eyes went wide and she drew in a deep, overly dramatic breath. "I beg your pardon." She laughed; a nervous, rapid chirp that typically signaled Armageddon.

Gene, Jean, Sammie, and Sonny, quickly and quietly exited the room along with Mr. Thomas. Meanwhile Abigail sat with arms stretched out on the back of the sofa, wearing a composed smirk, and delighting in the anticipation of witnessing the show of the century.

"You . . . called . . . Dooby?" Hannah questioned, placing her toe on that proverbial fine line.

Buford exchanged a knowing glance with his daughter then winked. "*I* talked to Dooby this morning, Hannah," he said sternly.

"Oh, for the love of Pete!" Hannah began, followed by the customary fanning and hyperventilating. "The two of you have conspired against me. You want me to join Nettie Mae, is that it? Delilah Leigh Beauregard, I won't stand for this! Do you know what people will say if that boy follows you to Oklahoma?"

Hannah's tirades always began this way. First, Pete (whoever that was) was acknowledged, and then the conspiracy element was introduced, followed by the full name of the tirade's intended target, and bringing up the rear, the over-used "what will people say." These rants typically went on for a solid ten to fifteen minutes before the caterwauling began.

In a flash Hannah advanced to pacing and wailing.

"Wow, that was quick," Delilah observed. Being accustomed to Hannah's melt-downs, Delilah and Buford looked on anticipating the next stage; wrath, apparently manifesting its ugly head more quickly than usual, as well.

"Don't you get smart with me, Missy," Hannah growled inhumanly as she tucked her purse under her arm with a jerk. "I'll be in the car, Buford."

Hannah turned with a snap and stormed toward the front door while Abigail, still smirking, rose from the sofa and followed her aunt.

"Mother," Delilah called out, chasing after Hannah.

The three women converged at the front door.

"I'm sorry, Mother," Delilah pleaded sincerely as Hannah's hand grasped the door knob. "I'm sorry that you're so upset about this. But I'm quite determined to see that this works."

Hannah turned slowly to face her daughter. Her eyes narrowed and flashed ire as a twisted smile crept across her face. "And I am quite determined to see that it does not," she hissed.

After Hannah's departure, Delilah was left standing in the entry hall with Abigail. Resisting the urge to slap the permanently affixed sneer off her cousin's face, Delilah smiled as Abigail leaned in toward Delilah and whispered in her ear. "You may as well know, Dear Cousin, should your mother fail at this endeavor, I shall not."

A month had passed without incident. No injunctions, threats or subpoenas; no fires, floods or stray bullets. Delilah's mother was still hibernating in her cone of silence, but Buford had been in touch; if Hannah was plotting an attack, Buford's watchful eye had not detected it. It wasn't Hannah that concerned Buford. He knew that in the end he could stop her; Abigail was a different story. Abigail's reputation for getting what she wanted, more often by sneaky, ruthless means than not, was legendary.

Since Delilah now owned Nettie Mae's 1996 Ford pickup, and her 1967 Camaro RS/SS 427, it seemed logical to sell the three year old BMW she owned in Macon. The condominium she owned was a different matter. Buford and Delilah agreed to lease the condominium, thereby allowing her a monthly income, and reserving a dwelling should her attempt at ranching prove unsuccessful. No doubt her purse would welcome the added weight, but she knew the extra funds were only a temporary fix to a long term issue.

Dooby had successfully delivered her personal belongings, and a few prized antique furniture pieces. Delilah, Dooby and Gus had spent a week incorporating Delilah's things with Nettie's things.

They combed through Nettie's clothes and personal items, separating them into stacks for keeping, or donating. They stowed what was kept in Rubbermaid containers and secured the containers in the barn.

Having vehemently refused Delilah's offer to stay in the guest bedroom, Dooby now called the unoccupied apartment over the two car garage, home. The argument had not been won by Dooby's concern about Delilah's reputation, or Hannah's reaction.

"Would you stop worrying about Mother?" Delilah pressed. "She will always protest your involvement in my life. And having a black man living in my home is the least of my worries."

"Delilah, a man got's to have his own space!" Dooby finally said.

"Oh, alright," Delilah capitulated. And with that, the two fixed-up and cleaned-up the small, one bedroom apartment, and filled it with the overflow of furniture from the house.

"Actually, this was a good idea," Delilah said as they pushed a chest of drawers into place. "It gives me a place to store things that can be put to use, and provides you with a man cave. I'm glad you thought of this, Dooby."

Dooby just grinned and shook his head.

With a shaved head, neatly trimmed mustache and goatee, and muscular, bronze body that stood just over six feet tall, Dooby had all the appearance of an intimidating night club bouncer. His disposition, on the other hand, was polar opposite. He was a quiet, humble, gentle man who preferred living simply and perfecting his craft; carpentry. And he was a brilliant carpenter. He could build or repair anything. His talents and hard work in addition to his mother's psychic abilities and accounting prowess had produced a small fortune; a fortune he happily shared with an ex-wife, and two daughters now in college. The only possessions he cherished were his truck and tools, and they had come with him to Oklahoma.

During the day, Gus continued Delilah's education of the ranching business, while Dooby set about mending fences, updating the plumbing, and tending to the multitude of small repairs to the house and barn. The three dined together in the big house each evening, and after the dishes were washed they went their separate ways, except on Thursday nights when Delilah attempted to teach the two men how to play poker.

"You guys are on your own tomorrow night," Delilah announced one evening over fried pork-chops. "I'm meeting Herbert in Cushing for dinner."

"So," Dooby teased. "You're on a first name basis with the attorney, and now you have a date with him."

"No! It's not a date." Delilah objected. "I'm sure he has some legal issues to discuss with me."

"Uh huh," Dooby said with a grin. "That's what they all say."

"Now there's the pot calling the kettle black," Delilah fired back. "You've been to Cushing three times in the past week. What's her name and when are you bringing her out here for supper? Or are you afraid I'll embarrass you?"

A broad smile stretched across Dooby's face, "Delilah, that boat sailed long ago."

"If I didn't know better," Gus said shaking his head. "I'd thwear you two were thiblingth."

"For all intents and purposes, we are," Dooby said with a chuckle. "And by the way, I'm going to Cushing tonight."

Cushing, the pipeline crossroads of the world, situated in the far southeast corner of Payne County, was fifteen minutes north the ranch; give or take a few minutes, depending on the route taken. The oil storage tanks that spotted the landscape south of town could be seen from the second floor of the ranch house.

The tank farms had grown in number since Delilah's childhood summer visits, along with the size of the tanks themselves; the largest holding a half million barrels. And now tank farm developments were springing up north of town, as well.

The three parted company. Gus went to his mobile home, Dooby set out for his rendezvous in Cushing, and Delilah had a date with a hot bubble bath, and a cup of tea. After the second cup of tea and a couple chapters of Harry Potter, she was fast asleep.

Early the following morning, as Delilah slowly became conscious of darkness giving way to light, she heard the all-too-familiar sound of chewing, and felt the all-too-familiar soft, moist touch upon her nose. She opened one eye to find the ghostly, gray eyes of Pandora staring back at her.

"Pandora!" Delilah moaned. "How do you do it? Am I going to have to stay up all night to find out how you get out of your pen and then into the house?"

Delilah threw the covers back and sat on the side of the bed. She reached out and scratched the goat between the ears. Pandora advanced, and began nudging her; each nudge becoming stronger and seemingly less friendly.

"Okay, you want an apple?" Delilah said with a laugh.

The goat turned and scampered toward the bedroom door. She stopped just as she reached the opening and looked back at Delilah, who followed the animal down the stairs and into the kitchen. With two apples in hand, Delilah led Pandora out the backdoor, and then tossed the fruit on the ground.

After a full day of menial household tasks, Delilah showered, and prepared for her non-date date with Herbert.

She twisted her long, black curls into a loose knot atop her head, applied a small amount of make-up to her face, shrugged into a hot pink, sweater and black slacks, and then slid her feet into a pair of black high heels.

Twenty minutes later she was met by a fidgeting Herbert in front of his office in Cushing.

Herbert was a lanky, awkward, and fashionably challenged man who always donned a red bow-tie and suspenders. His long, thinning, light brown hair swept from one ear, across the top of his head to the other ear, and he was forever pushing his wire rimmed glasses up the bridge of his nose.

The fifteen minute drive north on Highway 18 to the Stone Wolf Casino and Grill was filled with idle chit chat, interjected with personal queries. Being no stranger to first date protocol, Delilah found herself wondering if Dooby had been right, and this business meeting had nothing to do with business.

After the waitress had taken their order, Herbert suggested that Delilah join him in a game of golf the following day. Delilah pleasantly declined the invitation explaining that she'd had no interest in golf courses since the death of her first husband.

"He was killed by a flying golf cart," Delilah announced as nonchalantly as if she were reporting on the evening news.

Realizing the absurdity of the statement coupled with the bewildered expression on

Herbert's face, Delilah continued. "It all started when J. J. broke his leg skiing in Colorado. He loved to play golf, and after four weeks of restricted activities in a cast, a couple of his friends, one of which was an intern at the hospital, persuaded J. J. to join them on the golf course."

Herbert looked confused.

"Well, you see," Delilah forged ahead. "They strapped J. J. into a 'borrowed' wheelchair and then secured the wheelchair to the back of the golf cart. There didn't seem to be a problem until they were set to tee off on the fifteenth hole which was at the top of Devil's Crown; probably the highest point in three counties. Somehow the brakes failed on the golf cart and it began rolling down the hill.

"They said he probably would have been okay had the cart not hit some sort of obstruction in its path, and caused it to start tumbling end over end. The wheelchair came loose, but J. J. didn't. Eventually the cart landed on top of the wheelchair."

Delilah had become accustomed to the varied reactions she got when telling folks about the odd deaths of her five husbands. They seemed to be broken down into four groups; the mortified, the skeptics, the sympathizers, and the amused. Herbert, practically biting a hole in his lower lip, clearly fit into the last category.

"Herbert," Delilah began with a southern drawl sweeter than molasses. "I hope you'll forgive my bluntness, but I was under the impression you had business matters to discuss with me tonight."

"I do," he replied with a guilty grin. "But it doesn't have to be all business, does it?"

Herbert addressed the business matters as they drove back to Cushing. He advised Delilah that there had been several inquiries concerning the status of the ranch. All but one of the interested parties seemed content to drop their attempted acquisitions when the attorney explained the conditions of Delilah's inheritance, and the restrictions applying to the sale of the property. One, however, was not satisfied.

Murray Rockford was the son of Joseph Rockford. Joseph had owned the entire mile section where the Royal Flush Ranch now sat. He had lost half the parcel of land to Nettie in a poker game, along with the mineral rights and the house. From there, he drank and gambled the remaining property away, with the exception of five acres and a hovel, which sat in near ruin behind Delilah's property, and was currently occupied by Murray.

It was well known that Murray, in drunken stupors, vowed to get back his birth right by any means necessary. It was also no secret that Murray's brawn was far mightier than his brain, and his temper was equal to his brute strength.

"I'm afraid Murray Rockford did not take the news as well as the others," Herbert said, desperately trying to conceal his concern. "He's volatile and careless, which makes him exceptionally dangerous, Delilah. I have to admit I'm a little worried about you being on the ranch all alone."

"But I'm not alone," Delilah countered. "I have Dooby, and Gus . . . and Pandora."

She then conveyed the goat's propensity to escape her pen and attack strangers who'd ventured onto the property for whatever purpose, going as far as to trap Larry the lineman from the electric company at the top of a pole where he was repairing a security light.

"I got a call from the dispatcher asking me to remove the goat from the base of the pole," she said with a giggle. "Poor man. He was terrified. He told me they flagged accounts with bad dogs all the time, but he'd never flagged an account for a bad goat."

Delilah smiled at the memory unaware that Herbert had pulled in next to her pickup in front of his office. She thanked him for dinner, and they parted company with Herbert's borderline flirtatious promise he'd be in touch.

As she made her way south on Highway 99, and just a few miles prior to her turn off, her quiet contemplation was interrupted by the sudden and swift appearance of a vehicle behind her. It seemed they had come from nowhere; an unexpected apparition on a dark and lonely road. The driver advanced dangerously close to the rear of her pickup. Bright lights began flashing, momentarily blinding her. She checked the speedometer; sixty-five miles per hour. Aggravated by the reckless driver behind her, she was tempted to tap the brakes, but knew they were too close.

In an instant the driver swerved to the left as if attempting to pass her. Delilah slowed. Before she could get a good look at the vehicle or the man driving it, she realized that the nondescript truck was much too close to her pickup and she instinctually jerked the steering wheel to the right to avoid a collision.

Moments later, Delilah was in a ditch catching her breath and thanking The Maker she was still alive. Though she knew in her heart her assailant was long gone, she couldn't help but look up, in hopes of seeing something that could possibly identify him. To her horrified astonishment she discovered the man had turned around and was coming back toward her.

She turned the key to restart the pickup but nothing happened. The oncoming truck got closer and then slowly crossed the lane of traffic.

"Don't get out of the vehicle," she panted out loud, remembering one of Buford's many safety lectures. Her hand instantly went to the automatic door locks, and she pressed the button down as the other driver pulled his truck directly in front of her. She blinked feverishly at the bright lights, and held her left hand in front of her eyes while she frantically groped in her purse for her cell phone with her right hand. Her heart sank as she saw the driver's door on the opposing vehicle open.

Chapter 3

The Well House

As Delilah turned into her drive, and she made her way slowly up the winding lane to the house, she weighed the consequences of sharing with Dooby her terrifying experience. Knowing his propensity to shift into the role of over protective soul brother, resulting in her every action being watched and guarded to the extreme, she tended toward giving him only the Reader's Digest condensed version of the episode. After all, she couldn't be entirely certain the man who had forced her off the road had done so intentionally. It could just as easily have been an accident. She would never know. The mystery man had hastily departed the scene of the accident when a highway patrolman topped the hill behind her and engaged his emergency lights.

Before she even entered the back door of the house, she knew Dooby was patiently waiting inside, poised to interrogate her about the so called date with Herbert.

"So," he inquired with a confident smirk as he leaned against the kitchen cabinet. "How was your . . . date?"

"Yes, yes. I humbly concede you were right. Herbert may have had ulterior motives," Delilah answered with a roll of her eyes.

"You didn't have to crack him over the head or anything, did you?" he asked, relentlessly clinging to his amused expression.

Delilah laughed. "No! His intent was implied. He *did* have business to discuss with me, but it wasn't anything he couldn't have conveyed in five minutes over the phone."

Dooby's mood suddenly shifted from light and playful to dark and stern. "What else happened this evening?" he prodded.

Delilah knew an attempt to conceal the accident was futile. Unfortunately, Dooby knew her like a well read book, and he'd been reading her for years. On occasion, she had even suspected that he had inherited a bit of his mother's psychic abilities, though Dooby denied having such talents. She bit her lower lip, deciding what to tell and what not to tell.

"I had an accident," she blurted out, and then quickly added. "Nothing major. I just ran off the side of the road. A highway patrolman helped me out of the ditch."

"Are you okay?" Dooby asked with marked concern as he stepped toward her and began scrutinizing her face and arms.

After repeated assurances from Delilah, and another examination of her extremities, Dooby seemed moderately convinced of her well being. He hugged her tightly, kissed her forehead, bid her goodnight, and retreated to his simple domicile above the garage.

Morning came early. Dressed in blue jeans, a tee-shirt, and her inherited pair of worn-out work boots, Delilah descended the stairs. Her first stop was the kitchen where she started a pot of coffee. Within fifteen minutes Dooby was crossing the threshold of the back door.

"How do you feel this morning?" he asked as he poured a mug of brew for himself. "You sore?"

"Nope," Delilah trilled, refilling her cup.

There was a tap on the back door, instantly followed by the appearance of Gus.

"Morning Delilah . . . Dooby," Gus said with a nod as he made a bee line for the coffee pot. "Oh, Delilah, I think we have a problem with the well pump."

"You know, Gus, the word 'problem' has such a negative connotation," Delilah observed. "Let's just say we have a situation which requires a solution."

The toothless ranch hand stared at her incredulously, and then blinked. "A thituation which requireth a tholution?"

Delilah, void of expression, studied the man's face. "Okay, what's the problem?"

While Gus explained the "thticking thwitch" to Dooby, Delilah washed her coffee cup and then silently went over her list of things to do. It was going to be a busy week.

By week's end Delilah had evicted her encounter with the reckless driver from her thoughts. She had much more important things to dedicate to long term memory; such as Dooby's instructions on the new pump in the well house and how it operated.

"Pay attention, Delilah," Dooby scolded as he went through the directions a second time.

Delilah pulled her long, black curls away from her face, and focused intently on Dooby's verbal dissertation, but all she heard was, "Wah wah wah, electrical current, blah blah blah, switch, yadda yadda pump the water."

"I'm going to town," Delilah announced after the third go round. "I have to get groceries."

"Do you need money?" Dooby asked, reaching for the wallet in his back pocket.

"No," she quickly replied. "We're good."

And it was true. They were good for the time being. As she drove to Cushing, she mentally calculated her expenditures against her income. The month's expenses had been remunerated, and if she was mindful about her spending, the money she had received from the sale of her car would cover expenses for a few more months. Beyond that, she had no clue what she would do.

After purchasing her provisions, and loading them into the back of the pickup, she climbed in behind the wheel and started the truck. It was at this point she noticed a slip of paper that had been tucked under the windshield wiper. She retrieved the note and got back into the pickup. As she read the menacing words she was torn between fear and rage. *Your choice – walk away or be carried out in a pine box.*

Delilah stuffed the note in her purse. She scanned the parking lot quickly for any sign of the culprit who had placed the note on her windshield, but found nothing suspicious. She sat for a moment considering the list of those who would delight in her failure at the ranch. Surely Hannah would not be involved in anything that would result in bodily harm to her only daughter; though frightening her might be the objective. And then there was Abigail who was capable of anything. There was also Murray Rockford to consider, and the mystery man who ran her off the road earlier that week. Delilah wondered if they were one and the same or if she was being fired on from different directions.

"I can't think about that now. I'll think about it tomorrow," she said to herself, opting to 'Scarlett' that concern for the moment.

After supper that evening Delilah sat cross legged on the sofa going through a box of Nettie Mae's old pictures. Dooby entered the living room after cleaning the kitchen.

"I'm going to town," he announced "I think Gus went to the Senior Citizen's dance in Cushing. Are you going to be okay here, by yourself?"

"Of course I'll be okay," she answered, giving only fleeting regard to the note in her purse. And with that she waved him on and wished him a nice evening.

Within an hour she had sorted through the pictures and placed them in two stacks, those she was familiar with, and those she was not. One in particular she sat aside to share with Dooby.

It was a ten year old Dooby and a nine year old Delilah sitting on the back of a mare. The ranch foreman's young son, Eli, was holding the reigns. Dooby's larger-than-life afro might have been the center of attention had it not been completely overshadowed by the look of absolute terror in his saucer sized eyes. Delilah guffawed at the memory.

Feeling a wave of exhaustion Delilah decided to take a long, hot bubble bath and call it an early night. She went upstairs, corked the old claw-and-ball bathtub, and began running the water.

Within a couple minutes the faucet began sputtering and gurgling, and then the flow of water stopped altogether. Delilah tugged on the blue jeans she had just stepped out of, pulled her tee-shirt back over her head, and trekked down the stairs. As she reached the back door in the kitchen, she slipped her feet into a pair of Crocs, and grabbed the keys to the well house. She paused a moment, giving thought to what else she may need; a flashlight, just in case the entire well house was without power.

She exited the house, and made her way the thirty yards or so in the cold, crisp air, to the corner of the garage, and then proceeded past Pandora's pen to the well house and propane tank which sat an additional thirty yards beyond the back of the garage. The amber glow of the security light beamed brightly, giving her a clear view of the sleeping goat.

As she reached for the padlock on the door of the well house she was startled to find it was already unlocked; obviously an oversight on Dooby's part. She stuffed the keys in the pocket of her jeans and pushed the door open. She carefully reached around the door opening and found the light switch. The light came on, and she entered, relieved that the power problem was limited to the pump.

With her back to the partially opened door, she bent over the pump in the confined space to assess the cause of its failure, wishing she had paid closer attention to Dooby's instructions. Focused intently on the numerous parts, switches, and gizmos, her peripheral sight did not catch the shadow in the doorway until it was too late.

"Hey!" Delilah shouted as she lunged for the closing door. She heard the click of the padlock, and a low, creepy chuckle.

"Who's there?" she demanded.

She traced the sound of footsteps around to the side of the windowless well house. There was a quick, sharp snip, and she was plunged into total darkness. "Well, that can't be good," she said to herself in a low voice as she labored to maintain composure. Then she remembered the flashlight, and began groping for it. At the same time it occurred to her that the lock was outside but the key was in her pocket, making her location perhaps the safest place to be. Her fear gave way to relief, and then swiftly moved to anger. If the key was in her pocket, how would Dooby or Gus be able to get her out?

Her inner monologue was interrupted by a banging sound; metal on metal. It was coming from the propane tank. She jumped with fright as a high pitched hissing sound replaced the banging. Within seconds the man was standing outside the door of the well house. He said only one word.

"Boom!"

Pushing the envelope of safety, Dooby sped down the gravel road toward the ranch. He'd received an urgent call from his psychic mother, Vonda. Delilah was in peril once again. His heart sank as he topped a hill and saw an orange, fiery glow from the direction of the ranch.

Delilah was no stranger to mishaps, and Dooby had been witness to the greater part of them. He had pulled her from the freezing water of a pond after her failed attempt to skate on ice that was too thin. He had stepped between her and a rabid dog on the verge of attack. He had broken her fall from a ladder, receiving a fractured collar bone for his heroic effort. The list went on and on. She had always emerged relatively unscathed. He raced up the winding drive to the emergency vehicles grouped near the fire.

His eyes were searching for Delilah even before he screeched to a gravel-slinging halt, and bolted from the car. The Lincoln County Sheriff approached him with raised arms, and began interrogating him.

"Where's Delilah?" Dooby asked frantically, ignoring the sheriff's questions and pushing past him with brute force.

"I'm here, Dooby," she called out, as she ran toward him, Pandora in tow.

Dooby scooped Delilah into his arms. "Thank you, Sweet Jesus. Are you alright? What happened?" he fired away the questions, refusing to loosen his hold on her.

Having already explained to the sheriff the events that led up to her entrapment in the well house, Delilah conveyed the story to Dooby with tried patience.

"But . . . I don't understand. How did you get out?" Dooby asked, clearly confused.

"Well," Delilah began. "Since the door hinges were inside the well house, I used my keys as a sort of . . . chisel, and the Maglight as a hammer, and just dislodged the pins from the hinges. I couldn't get the door to budge so I called out to Pandora. Once I said the word 'apple' she was there. You know how she loves apples." Delilah rubbed the goats head with great affection, and then continued. "Anyway, she started butting the door, I assume with her head, and it gave way. We'd just made it to the other side of the garage when the propane tank blew."

Dooby stood in silent astonishment, shaking his head.

"It was really quick thinking on her part," the sheriff said.

"I don't know about that," Delilah said. "Honestly, I think faced with the prospect of incineration, anyone could be a MacGyver."

And then, much to Delilah's chagrin, the sheriff asked for the threatening note that had been placed on her windshield earlier that day. The explosion of the propane tank paled in comparison to the fireworks that occurred following the sheriff's request. Dooby was livid that Delilah had withheld that bit of information from him.

"Great," Delilah said in a low voice to the sheriff, as Dooby ranted to the cool, night air. "I won't even be able to go to the bathroom now without someone standing guard outside the door."

The sheriff grinned sheepishly. "Sorry."

Two days later, Dooby and Gus sat at the kitchen table with morning coffee cups in hand, reading the local newspapers while Delilah looked on with feigned disinterest. Dooby was finally speaking to Delilah, but his body guard mentality hadn't waned in the slightest.

"Was there anything in the newspaper about the explosion?" Delilah asked cautiously.

"Just a little blurb on the third page." Dooby replied.

Delilah had come to loath newspapers; having had the mysterious deaths of five husbands headlined along with the implications of her involvement in said deaths. "DEATH BY CHOCOLATE" was the most absurd headline of all.

It was rumored that the eccentric mother of Delilah's third husband lived on nothing but chocolate while pregnant. Consequently, no one was surprised when she named her infant son Hershey. Even less surprising was his chosen career path; a candy maker or chocolatier as he preferred. While perfecting his cocoa cookies for canines, one of the mechanical arms in the small factory malfunctioned and hit Hershey in the back, knocking him into a large vat of boiling chocolate. And alas, Mrs. Hershey Smith, AKA

Delilah Leigh Beauregard Hamilton Fisher, was widowed once more. It was at this point the whispers of "Black Widow" began spinning in the web of society.

Delilah sprung from her seat excitedly as she remembered her activities two nights prior. She raced to the living room and returned with a picture in hand.

"I forgot all about this, Dooby," she said, sliding to a stop beside him and handing him the Polaroid image. "I found this night before last when I was going through all the pictures. Remember the summer you came here with me when we were kids?"

Dooby laughed heartily. He handed the picture to Gus, who looked at the picture, then looked at Delilah, then looked at the picture again, and then back at Dooby.

"Delilah, you haven't changed a bit," Gus said. Slowly the corners of his mouth turned up. "Now Dooby, you're a different thtory." The scrawny, bug-eyed boy with a monstrous afro, sitting on the back of the mare with Delilah, looked nothing like the muscular Adonis with NO hair, sitting beside him at the table.

"Who'th thith?" Gus asked pointing to the boy holding the horse's reigns.

"Eli," Delilah answered without looking at the picture. "Eli Simmons . . . Simons, something like that."

"That'th Eli?" Gus questioned with astonishment.

"You know Eli?" Delilah and Dooby said in unison.

Gus explained the story conveyed to him by Nettie. At eight years old, Eli, who was a couple years older than Delilah, had moved to the ranch with his father after being abandoned by his mother. Tragically, his father, who had been the ranch foreman, passed away when the boy was sixteen. Nettie took the boy under her wing; having been unsuccessful in locating Eli's mother, and continued to raise him. She then sent him to Oklahoma State University where he studied geology, received his master's degree, and now traveled the world as one of the country's top geologists. Gus had met Eli the last time he visited the area.

"You know," Delilah said contemplatively. "I stopped spending summers here about the time his dad past away. I had no idea. No one ever told me Eli's story, and I never asked. I feel bad about that."

Delilah looked at the picture and smiled. "Who'd have guessed such a mean, spiteful, little boy could make good," she said with a chuckle.

"What are you talking about?" Dooby said inquisitively. "He wasn't mean."

"I beg to differ," Delilah protested. "He was always pinching me, tugging my hair, calling me names and pulling pranks on me, when he wasn't boring me to tears with the triviality of rocks."

Dooby laughed. "Yeah, that's what eleven year old boys do to get the attention of nine year old girls they're smitten with."

Gus nodded in agreement while Delilah stood with perplexity written all over her face.

After returning the picture to the living room, Delilah joined Gus and Dooby at the water well, where Dooby had already framed the new well house. The explosion had destroyed only the propane tank, well house and pump. Mercifully, the well itself had not been affected.

For several hours the three measured, sawed and hammered the new well house into existence. This time a window was added in the event an escape should ever be necessary.

The new propane tank was delivered and set into place, and by day's end one could scarcely tell that an explosion and raging fire had consumed the previous occupants of the same space.

"You're really good with a thaw," Gus told Delilah as they put away the power tools.

"Thanks," she said with smile. "I love power tools. Dooby taught me everything I know."

"Well, I don't know about everything," Dooby said. "But, I will take some credit for your knowledge of tools. Don't sell yourself short, though. You had a sincere eagerness to learn."

"Born out of necessity," Delilah added. "My business required it."

The following morning, Dooby and Gus sat at the kitchen table, sipping their coffee and exchanging fidgety, nervous glances at each other. Dooby requested that an extra plate be sat at the dinner table that night, and when Delilah inquired who would be joining them, Dooby announced that it was time they met Karon, his "friend" from Cushing.

After dancing and squealing with delight, Delilah stopped cold and addressed the two restless men. "What's up with you two?" she demanded.

Again, Dooby and Gus exchanged a cautious glance at each other. "I think it's time you learn to shoot a gun," Dooby said dryly.

Delilah put her hand to Dooby's forehead. "Are you ill? Have you taken a fall and hit your head?" she asked with genuine concern.

"No," he answered as though the question had not been rhetorical.

"Well then, you have completely taken leave of your senses? You honestly think putting a firearm in my hands is a good idea," she stated, more as fact than an inquiry.

Ten minutes later the three stood in the middle of a clearing between the barn and a grove of pecan and oak trees. A target had been placed in the center of a round bale of hay which had been strategically placed at the end of the clearing in front of a thicket of sand plum trees. It appeared that Gus and Dooby had given this venture careful consideration, even going so far as to move the livestock to the pasture at the other end of the property.

Dooby placed Nettie's .45 Ruger in Delilah's hand after a brief lesson in gun safety and a demonstration on lining up the sight of the gun with the target. He stepped back beside Gus and told her to pull the trigger.

She closed her eyes, instinctually fearing the noise, and squeezed the trigger. As soon as the gun fired she opened her eyes and followed the decent of a turkey vulture as it plummeted from the sky.

"Damn, did I do that?" she asked in horror.

Two hours, four dozen rounds of ammo, a perforated barn, and several barkless tree-trunks later, Delilah's two exasperated, exhausted instructors stood scratching their heads.

"You know, Dooby," Gus began. "Pepper thpray can be very effective, and ith a perfectly actheptable alternative."

"You may be on to something, Gus," Dooby said, pondering the suggestion intently. "Her assailant would have to be pretty close, though. The whole idea of the gun was to take them out before they got too close."

"True," Gus agreed. "But what elth will she take out in the protheth?"

On the verge of being offended, Delilah through her hands into the air and declared as she waved the gun, "Look, I never thought this was a good idea in the first place."

"Delilah, did you put the gun on safety?" Dooby asked with some urgency; his eyes fixed on the flailing weapon.

"I think so," she said as she lowered the Ruger to examine it.

The gun fired, Delilah jumped, and then she shrieked as she watched one of the men crumble to the ground.

Chapter 4

Karon

Delilah, Dooby and Gus were gathered in the emergency room at the hospital. Gus was remarkably content and jovial for someone who'd just been shot. No doubt his "happy" was in direct proportion to the massive dose of pain killers administered by the doctor. The bullet through his foot had mercifully and miraculously missed bones. The injured limb, now rapped in bandages, dangled over the edge of the examination table, and Gus was being amused by a "talking" tongue suppressor.

"I can't believe you shot Gus," Dooby said with a disbelieving shake of his head, and a roll of his sepia eyes.

"Oh, really?" Delilah countered sarcastically. "What DID you expect; that I'd channel the spirit of Annie Oakley after a mere two hours of instruction?"

Gus laughed and then pointed his gun shaped hands at the tongue suppressor and, with sound effects and all, began shooting.

There was a tap on the door followed by the entrance of the Lincoln County Sherriff. Gus aimed his finger-guns at the sheriff and told him to draw. The sheriff chuckled and then expressed relief that the lanky, toothless ranch hand had not been mortally wounded. After a brief interrogation, the sheriff was satisfied that the incident had been an accident. Filing charges would not be necessary. However, they would need to come to the office the next day to sign the report. He then recommended other options of self-defense for Delilah.

"I have never been so embarrassed in all my life," Delilah declared the instant the sheriff left the room.

"Seriously?" Dooby questioned in earnest. "What about the time you set Mary Lou Windom's veil on fire at her wedding?"

Delilah winced and shrugged.

"Oh," Dooby continued. "And then there was the time in the Junior Miss Georgia pageant when you were caught trying to gorilla glue Annie Kabowski's tutu to her toe shoes."

"She had that coming," Delilah said defensively. "She was a vicious little troll. And by the way, that would have worked if my fingers hadn't stuck to the tutu first. Gus, it's probably not safe for you to dance on top of the table." Delilah said as Gus attempted a pirouette on his good foot.

She turned to Dooby. "See if you can get him down from there before he breaks a bone. I'm going to the billing department."

When the three stooges arrived at the ranch, and Delilah and Dooby got Gus settled in the overstuffed chair, and his foot properly elevated on the ottoman, and his cherry Dr. Pepper made, and the television remote control within reach, Delilah set about preparing dinner for the three of them, plus their expected dinner guest, Karon.

Delilah had just finished setting the dining room table with her finest china and silver when she saw Dooby's pick-up inching up the drive. She tossed her long, black curls, fluffed the ruffles of her peacock blue blouse, brushed the flour from her black slacks, and with overwhelming anxiety quickly made her way to the back door to greet the couple.

Karon stood about five foot, six inches tall and was attractively plump; exactly Dooby's type. Her mocha latte skin was smooth and flawless, and her cherub like face was accentuated with dimples and sparkling black eyes.

"Karon, this is Delilah," Dooby said. "Delilah, this is Karon."

The space between Karon's eyebrows narrowed, and she perched her fisted hands on her hips. "THIS is your lifelong friend?" she asked, clearly incensed. "THIS is who you're stayin' with? She's a woman! She's a white woman! She's a beautiful, white woman. You didn't tell me you were livin' with a white woman."

"Well, I don't actually live with Delilah," Dooby said with a mischievous smile. "I live in the apartment over the garage."

Delilah slapped Dooby's arm. "Why didn't you tell her? You always do this and it causes nothing but trouble. I'm very pleased to meet you, Karon," Delilah said with her silkiest southern drawl as she took hold of Karon's arm. "Would you come with me to the living room? I'd like you to meet Gus, our ranch hand. He would have greeted you at the door too, but I shot him this morning and he really shouldn't be walking right now."

Karon's eyes went wide, whether with fear or admiration is uncertain, but then she smiled and said, "I think I'm gonna like you."

The conversation at dinner was light and inquisitive, and eventually segued to Delilah's love life. As is natural for most women, Karon was curious about it; had she met anyone special in Oklahoma yet, did she leave someone behind in Georgia, had she ever been married?

"Five times," Dooby said nonchalantly. "They all died."

Once again Karon's surprise was expressed in wide eyes, and she found it difficult to swallow the bite she had just taken. Sensing Karon's intrigue, Delilah began the account of being widowed five times. She explained how her first husband had been killed by an airborne golf cart, her second husband was stung by a bee on the day of his inauguration as Governor of Georgia, and hubby number three had died after falling into a vat of boiling chocolate. Karon interrupted the tale by means of a raised hand. She shook her head and asked how it was that Delilah had never been arrested.

"Oh, that was husband number four," Dooby said with a grin.

Unlike the three husbands that preceded him, Delilah's fourth husband, Cade Conner, was a race car driving, bungee jumping, sky diving daredevil, nine years her junior. Delilah theorized that if she married a younger man who was already reckless he would not be as likely to meet with an untimely death.

Six months after their "I do's" Cade slipped in the shower, hit his head, and drowned. And, unlike the previous three deaths, Delilah was indicted for murder, coincidentally falling on the heels of rejecting the advancements of the District Attorney. The subsequent trial was labeled a "judicial circus" by the media, who, by all accounts, played their parts as circus clowns quite convincingly. Delilah was exonerated, and the District Attorney was "persuaded" to resign his post. And so, Delilah's cougar period ended as quickly as it had begun.

Dooby's cell phone rang. A glowing smile stretched across his face as he read the name of the caller. "Hey, Boo," he said into the phone as he stood and started for the living room.

"Dooby's oldest daughter, Cassidy," Delilah said, addressing the curious look on Karon's face. "She's graduating from The University of Georgia end of this month, and then going into pre-med."

Karon nodded. "He has two daughters, right?"

Delilah beamed as she described the two girls who could not be more different. Cassidy was the epitome of the first born, over-achiever; Delaney was easy going. Cassidy looked like a super model; Delaney was the shorter, plumper, cute one. Cassidy had the mind of a brain surgeon; Delaney struggled to maintain a B average. Cassidy had the ambition of a hungry wolf;

Delaney was as enterprising as a snail. From birth, Cassidy had known no failure, and her cool, sophistication had garnered the respect of all those she came in contact with; Delaney had seen her share of disappointment, and her quick-witted, sassiness had made her the center of attention. Cassidy was perfect and perfectly boring; Delaney was beautifully flawed and immensely entertaining.

"You favor the youngest one, don't you?" Karon asked.

"No!" Delilah said. "Well, yes. I guess I do, but only because she's far more relatable. It's hard not to feel like a complete idiot around Cassidy. That child just thinks on a whole different level than most folks.

"I don't mean to keep staring at you, Karon," Delilah said, steering the conversation in another direction. "But you have the most beautiful skin. I've always envied women of color. It's so exotic and warm."

"Thank you," Karon said. "I was just thinking how pretty your skin is. It's just so . . . white."

"I wish I could tan," Delilah offered. "The sun burns me to a crisp, and the one and only time I used a tanning bed I came out looking like an albino Oompa Loompa."

Dooby returned to the laughter filled dining room, took his seat, and inquired as to what he'd missed. When Karon relayed the Oompa Loompa comment, Dooby grinned, nodded and confirmed that it was indeed, a hideous site.

"Well?" Delilah finally said, addressing Dooby.

"Next week," he answered, concentrating more on his apple cobbler than Delilah.

"Are you driving or flying?" she asked.

"Neither," he replied.

Delilah looked puzzled, and after a short stretch of silence she said, "Okay, you can't swim back to Georgia, so the only other alternatives would be taking a train or walking."

"I'm not going back," Dooby said. "There's too much going on here. I can't leave you unprotected."

"Oh, yes you can," Delilah said with determination. "And you will. Your oldest daughter is graduating from college, and under no circumstances are you going to miss that."

"Well then, you're coming back to Macon with me," Dooby said.

"Dooby, I can't go back with you," she argued. "Who'll take care of this place while Gus is incapacitated? Who'll take care of Gus?"

"Can we talk about this later?" Dooby said with controlled force.

"No! We'll talk about it right now," Delilah answered just as forcefully.

Dooby lowered his fork on the table with a thud. He glared at Delilah. It was a look he rarely used, but one that always resulted in Dooby having his way.

"There are two options, Delilah Leah Beauregard," he said in a calm but firm voice. "I'm staying here or you're coming with me. What'll it be?"

"I shouldn't have let you talk me into this," Dooby said, as he and Delilah stood beside his truck at dawn a week later. "It just doesn't feel right leaving you here."

"Look, Gus is staying in the house with me until his foot heals," Delilah said. "And you've arranged for the sheriff's department to make regular checks on me. Don't deny it. I overheard you talking to him. Now, go. I've got the work of two men to do."

Dooby embraced Delilah, and kissed the side of her head. He climbed into his pickup, started it, and rolled his window down while reciting the list of instructions he'd already given her three times before; keep the cell phone charged, keep the doors locked, be careful and ever mindful of her surroundings.

He paused a moment in deep thought. "Don't drive the car while I'm away," he said. And then, as if reading her unspoken objections, he quickly added. "You don't have the best of luck with vehicles, Delilah. And that's not a car you can simply replace if you wreck it."

Delilah's knowledge of automobiles extended no further than how and where to put the gasoline, but what she did know about Aunt Nettie's 1967 Camaro RS/SS 427 convertible was that her aunt had special ordered the car with extra packages, and over the past forty years every man she knew either drooled or hyperventilated at the mention of it. Now it sat in the double car garage at the Royal Flush Ranch covered with a lamb's wool blanket made especially for it.

"Love you, sista," Dooby said.

"Love you, too," Delilah replied. "Be careful, and hug the girls for me when you get there."

Delilah waved as Dooby drove down the winding drive. When nothing but a trail of dust could be seen, an eerily vulnerable feeling washed over her. She looked around, sensing she was being watched. "Get a grip, Delilah," she told herself.

That evening, after a full ten hours of hard labor, Delilah warmed a can of soup, and after serving Gus his portion, she stood at the kitchen sink, finished off the pot, and then went upstairs to shower. Just as she emerged from the shower, the landline rang. Her first thought was that Dooby had tried her cell phone, and when he didn't get an answer, he called the house phone.

"I was in the shower," she panted, as she answered the phone beside her bed.

"Thanks for that bit of info," the creepy voice said. "I'm more excited about your bodyguard being gone." And then there was a click.

It took Delilah about five minutes to squelch the nausea bubbling in the pit of her stomach. But once she did, she hustled down the stairs. She stopped first to make sure the front door was locked. She made her way to the French doors from the dining room to the screened porch and checked them, and then she slid to a finish at the back door where she clicked the deadbolt into the locked position.

She composed herself and went to the living room where Gus sat upright in wide-eyed terror. "Ith thomething wrong?" he asked.

"No," Delilah answered with a forced calm. "I just forgot to lock the back door, that's all. I meant to ask you earlier, Gus, did anyone call today?"

"Yeah," Gus answered. "The insuranth adjuthter. I wrote hith number down."

Delilah took the piece of paper from Gus, thanked him, and went back upstairs.

The following morning, after breakfast was eaten, and the dishes were washed, and a load of laundry was started, Delilah tended to Gus's foot and got him settled for another day of boob-tube watching.

She plopped down at the old, oak desk and called the insurance adjuster, who informed her that the claim for the propane tank and well house had been denied, and offered to send her the forms necessary to appeal the decision if she chose to do so. She agreed, and with a heavy sigh, she hung up.

Delilah had used practically every cent she had to pay for the new well house and propane tank with the expectation of reimbursement from the insurance company. She knew the rent money from her condo in Macon would not cover all the expenses coming due in just a couple weeks. She sat for a moment contemplating her quandary. If she had learned anything over the years, she'd learned that worry accomplished nothing, and if she channeled that energy into action, not only would there be a solution to the problem but the worry itself would be significantly diminished.

She called her attorney, Herbert, explained the situation, and suggested that the threat of litigation might possibly expedite the reimbursement process. He offered to come to the ranch that evening to go over her options. She agreed.

That evening, after sending Gus upstairs to shower, Herbert and Delilah sat comfortably on the living room sofa, positioned in the middle of the room, facing the fireplace. Herbert advised Delilah that even though the terms of Aunt Nettie's will prohibited her selling what she had inherited, it did not apply to the items forfeited by the others.

Delilah considered this new and unexpected revelation. She couldn't sell the stud horse, Henry's Last Hoorah, because he was the primary source of income for the ranch, though it had been some time since his last . . . job. She was too sentimentally attached to the Alexandrite brooch, and she didn't feel she was desperate enough to part with the Renoir, as yet.

"I have the perfect solution to your financial issues," Herbert said. He took hold of Delilah's hand and looked longingly into her eyes. He waited as though anticipating a response. Unfortunately, the only response he received was the look of total bewilderment. He shifted his body closer to hers. A small gasp sounded as Delilah filled her momentarily unused lungs, and her eye brows shot skyward.

"Marry me," he whispered.

"No!" she replied without hesitation. She wrenched her hand from his and pushed herself clear of him.

"Why not?" he whined, as he reached to take her hand again.

"I don't love you!" she exclaimed, leaning away from his advancement.

"What does that have to do with anything?" he pleaded, as he pushed his wire-rimmed glasses up the bridge of his nose. Delilah jumped up and took a couple steps backward toward the end of the sofa. Herbert began crawling on the sofa toward her. Her eyes went wide with panic, and she maneuvered around the end table and stood in the open space between the back of the sofa and the doorway.

"Herbert," she said incredulously. "I have never married a man I didn't love. And I'm not about to start now. Please, sir, contain your emotions!"

Herbert advanced in her direction over the back of the sofa. As he did, the sofa began teetering. Realizing the consequences of his actions, Herbert attempted to shift his weight to compensate for the imbalance. But it was too late. The sofa tipped over and landed with a thunderous boom, sending Herbert's lanky limbs flailing in all directions.

Just then, Gus came hobbling down the stairs wearing only a towel around his waist, and carrying the only weapon he could obtain on such short notice; a lamp from the bedside table in the guest bedroom. Delilah's cell phone rang.

It was Dooby. Delilah made a slashing motion at her neck with her hand as she glared at the two men in the living room. When Dooby asked how everything was, she lied.

She couldn't tell him about Herbert's odd proposal because then she'd have to explain the recently acquired money issues. She couldn't say anything about the creepy phone call the night before because he'd worry, or worse, he'd head back to Oklahoma and miss his daughter's graduation. So, she put on a happy face and told him everything was hunky-dory. And he bought it.

The following morning a profusely apologetic Herbert called and begged Delilah not to let his momentary lapse of good judgment affect their business relationship. With Herbert's solemn promise that such behavior would never be repeated, Delilah graciously forgave him and Herbert's confidence was restored.

Four days later, Delilah was quickly approaching the end of her rope. The days were getting warmer, Gus was getting antsier, Delilah was falling behind on the chores, and Pandora, the goat, was acting like a neglected, petulant child. Twice, Delilah had ended her day cleaning up a kitchen wrecked by the four legged creature.

It was the middle of the fifth day, when Delilah threatened to abscond with Gus's pain pills for her own consumption, the toothless ranch hand suggested he'd recovered sufficiently to move back to his mobile home and return to work the following morning. With that declaration, Delilah delivered Gus and his few belongings to his humble abode.

Delilah spent the remainder of the day on the tractor brush hogging. When daylight gave way to dusk, and she could no longer see sufficiently, she parked the tractor in the barn and walked the hundred yards of gravel lane back to the house. As she neared the back door she ran her hand in her jeans pocket for the house keys. No house keys.

"Great," she said out loud. Conjuring recollection, she saw in her mind's eye the key on the kitchen counter by the back door where she'd left it earlier that day. She knew the front door was locked, as well as the French doors. She turned the handle on the back door; sure enough it was locked, too. Her only option for entrance appeared to be through a window.

Procuring a chair from the patio and placing it under the kitchen sink window, Delilah began the process of breaking and entering her own home. Dishes rattled in the drain rack, and metal canisters clanked to the floor as she slithered through the opening.

The house was dark except for a faint sliver of muted light coming from the half bath off the downstairs hall. She made a mental note to leave the light on over the sink in the future. She got to her feet and groped toward the light switch near the door to the hall.

Just as she reached for the switch, a hand grabbed hers. She shrieked with fright and within seconds the man had twisted her arm behind her, and a blade was at her throat.

"Don't make a sound," he said.

Chapter 5

Eli

"Don't make a sound," the man said again, as he twisted Delilah's arm tighter behind her back.

Delilah stood perfectly still. For some reason, call it instinct, madness, or sheer stupidity, she wasn't frightened. This wasn't the voice of Mr. Creepy who'd locked her in the well house, and called her the day Dooby left. Oddly enough, this voice sounded absent of malice. And the unknown man was wearing very expensive cologne. But, what did she know about the voice and personal hygiene of a criminal? After all, he did have a knife at her throat. That had to count for something.

He lowered the knife, flipped on the kitchen light, and released Delilah's arm in one fluid move. Delilah turned slowly to face her attacker. A broad smile gradually crept across the man's face.

"Delilah?" he said with recognizing surprise.

"I beg your pardon, Sir. Do I know you?"

"Sorry about that," he said, walking to the back door. "I thought you were an intruder. I knew it wasn't Nettie, because she knows where the extra key is." He opened the back door and reached above the door facing. He brought his hand down and showed Delilah the key, and then returned it to its hiding place. "Evidently, you didn't. Where is Nettie, anyway?"

"Excuse me, Sir," Delilah said with less fear and more outrage. "Will you please identify yourself?"

"I'm thinking it may be more fun to keep you guessing," he said with a flirtatious glint in his jade green eyes.

And with that, it hit her. "Eli?" she exclaimed.

Eli nodded.

"Oh my goodness!" she exclaimed as she stepped toward him with open arms. Without hesitation Eli embraced her, and they began laughing. For a fleeting moment Delilah was caught off guard by a totally unexpected, but all too familiar, charge of attraction. She giggled nervously and stepped back from him.

"It's been a long time," she said.

"Almost thirty years," he offered. "The last time we were on the ranch at the same time, I was . . . what, fifteen and you were thirteen? We always seemed to miss each other's coming and going after that. You haven't changed much."

"Well the same cannot be said of you," she said with a smile. "You're all grown up. I hardly recognized you."

Delilah stood transfixed on Eli. He was no longer the scrawny, freckle-faced, boy with curly, strawberry blonde hair and buck teeth. He had matured into a tall, rugged man with broad shoulders. His short curls had darkened slightly, and his seductive smile revealed teeth that he had either grown into, or had been masterfully crafted by a very gifted dentist.

"So where's Nettie?" he asked again.

"Uh," Delilah stammered as she grasped for the right words. "Aunt Nettie passed away a couple months back."

"Oh," Eli said as all the playfulness drained from his face. He took a few steps back and leaned against the cabinets. "I . . . didn't know. What happened?"

"Pretty sure it was a heart attack," Delilah said.

There was an uncomfortable moment of silence in which Delilah assumed Eli was grieving. Eli was the first to break the silence.

"She was the closest thing to a mother I ever knew. I always told her I'd take care of her in her old age," he said with a hint of a chuckle. "She always said she would never get old."

Eli's tone darkened. "You said, 'pretty sure it was a heart attack.' Did they do an autopsy?" he asked.

"No," Delilah replied. "Why would you ask that?"

"Never mind," he said, still deep in thought. "She had some problems with the son of the previous owner of the ranch."

"Murray," Delilah guessed.

"Yeah," Eli agreed. "You know him? Has he been giving you trouble, too?"

"No," Delilah said. She winced and shook her head. "Well, I can't say for certain it's him. I mean . . . I don't know who it is.

"How did you get here?" Delilah asked quickly. "I didn't see a vehicle in the drive."

"I parked it in the garage," he replied. "I always park in the garage when I come home. I hope that's not a problem." He paused a moment, and then with a look of surprised comprehension he added, "Oh, this is awkward. If you're uncomfortable with me staying here, I can make other arrangements."

After a split second's consideration, Delilah replied, "No. You don't need to make other arrangements. I mean . . . in all fairness the house is as much yours as it mine."

"So, she left the ranch to you," Eli said.

"Yes, she did," Delilah concurred. "I sometimes wonder what she was thinking."

Eli nodded and smiled. "I learned a long time ago not to question Nettie's motives. Her decisions and advice seemed crazy at times, but in the end she was always right."

The two adjourned to the living room and got comfortable on the sofa, where they spent over three hours catching up on the past thirty years. Eli shared his world travels with Delilah, and Delilah briefed Eli on her five husbands and their odd and untimely deaths. Eli showed no evidence of shock, amusement or sympathy, which led Delilah to believe that her Aunt Nettie had already filled him in on the particulars.

The following morning, with a small jolt of excitement at the thought of her house guest, Delilah bolted from her bed, showered, and paid a bit more attention to hair and make-up than usual. Opting not to guild the lily, she dressed in blue jeans and her best t-shirt. She went downstairs to the kitchen and began making breakfast for Gus and Eli who were conspicuously absent.

As she tended to the meal, she stole numerous glances out the kitchen window, watching for the two men to come from the barn, and it occurred to her that Eli must have replaced the screen she had removed the night before when she was forced to climb through the window.

Her cell phone rang and she was delighted to see that it was Dooby calling.

"You're never going to believe who showed up here last night," Delilah said excitedly into the phone, after she patiently listened to Dooby's updates.

"Who?" Dooby asked with a hint of concern in his voice.

"Eli!" Delilah exclaimed. "Dooby, he's so different. Not at all like he was when we were children. It amazes me how such an awkward, irritating little boy could turn into such a fine man."

"Now, Delilah," Dooby cautioned, "it wasn't that long ago you vowed you'd never again become involved with a man who traveled."

Indeed, this declaration had come upon the death of Delilah's fifth and last husband, Jeremy Smith. As it turned out, the successful, aerospace parts salesman and extensive traveler was also a bigamist with two other wives; a fiery redhead with a temper who lived in Seattle, and a sweet, quiet blonde who lived in Houston.

The blonde was serving twenty five years to life for shooting Jeremy, the redhead had taken all his money, and Delilah was left with nothing more than his accumulated frequent flyer miles, and the expense of committing the man's remains back to the earth.

Fortunately, the expense of his burial was minimal having already purchased a double plot and headstone with the name SMITH on it, after the death of husband number three. The joke at Cavender's Funeral Home was that Delilah may not have killed two Smiths with one stone, but she certainly buried two Smiths with one.

"For heaven's sake. Who said anything about getting involved?" she said defensively.

"You can't fool me, Delilah Leigh Beauregard. I've been down this road with you too many times. Is he married?"

"I don't know!" Delilah said with a hint of annoyance.

"You mean you didn't ask him?"

"Oh, that should be a pleasant conversation, 'by the way, Eli, you don't happen to have a wife . . . or TWO hangin' around, do you?'"

Dooby laughed.

"Oh!" Delilah said urgently, as she peeked out the window one more time. "Here they come. I'll talk to you later."

"It got blown up," Gus said to Eli, as the two men came through the back door and sat at the kitchen table. "Didn't Delilah tell you?"

Delilah shot Gus a warning glare as she placed their plates of eggs and bacon in front of them, but Gus trudged on with an accounting of the numerous mishaps since Delilah's arrival; the threatening note left on her pickup, and the propane tank and well house explosion at the hands of Mr. Creepy. He went on to explain that the expense of replacing the propane tank and well house had left The Royal Flush Ranch in a bit of a pinch financially.

"Gus!" Delilah finally said. "That's enough. Let's not burden Eli with all our problems."

The look of astonishment and concern on Eli's face was replaced by one of purpose. Eli rose from his chair and began rummaging in the back of the top shelf of the pantry.

"Every time I returned from my travels," Eli began. "I would do various odd jobs around here to help Nettie out. And every time she insisted on paying me. Cash. I couldn't keep the money, and she damn sure wouldn't keep it herself. So," he pulled a small wooden box from the abyss, and opened it.

"Aunt Nettie's recipe box!" Delilah exclaimed. "I've been looking all over for that."

Extracting a wad of bills from the box, Eli concluded. "I put the money in here." He extended his overflowing hands toward Delilah. "Take it, Delilah."

Before Delilah could object, Eli pressed on. "I assure you, I don't need the money, Delilah. It was meant for a rainy day. And from the sounds of it, it's pouring around here."

With a smile, a nod, and a voice just above a whisper, she thanked him.

Eli excused himself and went to the living room. Delilah sat down at the table and counted out the money. She sighed and patted Gus' arm.

"It looks like you'll get a paycheck at least for the next few months, Gus."

"I wasn't worried about it, Delilah," he said.

"I know. But I was," she said as she cleared the breakfast dishes from the table.

Twenty minutes later Eli returned to the kitchen and announced he had contacted two ranchers in Arkansas and made arrangements to deliver Henry's Last Hoorah for stud service the following week. And when he informed Delilah of the amount she would receive for stud fees, she knew, barring any explosions or other catastrophes, her money issues had been resolved for at least another year.

That evening after dinner, Delilah received a call from Karon. She suspected Dooby had asked Karon to check on her, though Karon denied it. She had called to invite Delilah to join her, and her friends that weekend for an evening of nickel ante poker. Delilah accepted without hesitation, crediting her over exposure to high doses of testosterone, and the need for an evening filled with estrogen.

"I have a new house guest," Delilah informed Karon, as she sat cross legged on her bed. "His name is Eli. For all intents and purposes, he was raised here on the ranch. So, technically, I suppose he's more like a temporary roommate than a house guest."

"And what's he doing there now?" Karon asked suspiciously.

Delilah gave Karon the condensed version of Eli's story. "He's a geologist. He travels the world collecting rocks. He stays on the ranch between jobs."

"Is he a good lookin' man?" Karon asked eagerly.

"Karon!" Delilah shrieked. "What does that have to do with anything?"

"That bad, huh?" Karon said.

"No!" Delilah contradicted. "He's . . . cute, I guess. Fair haired, light eyes and a smile that could melt stone."

"Mmm hmm," Karon said. "I can't wait to meet him. How long is he staying?"

"I'm not sure," Delilah answered. "We haven't discussed that."

Delilah concluded her call and joined Eli in the living room. There were several issues that hadn't been discussed; issues that required answers. At the top of the list was Eli's personal life; more specifically, his marital status. She struggled with her desire to know more while not appearing to be too solicitous with her inquiry.

She plopped down on the sofa and remained quiet until Eli's attention was drawn away from the book he was reading.

"So, Eli," she began nervously. "Tell me more about your life for the past thirty years."

Eli put his book down, looked at Delilah, cocked his head to one side, and with a sly grin said, "What do you want to know?"

"Well," Delilah said, knowing full well that he knew where she was going with this line of questioning and knowing she had gone too far to turn back. "Have you ever been married? Are you married now? Or do you just have a girl in every port?"

The moment she asked these questions she was reminded of how absolutely inept she was at subtlety. She didn't need the long stretch of silence or the look of utter amusement on Eli's face to confirm the point.

After taking his sweet time toying with her, he finally answered. "Yes, no, and no." He said. He picked up his book and smiled.

"Details, Eli!" she said with exasperation.

He laughed. "Her name is Gabriella. She is, or was, a Brazilian model, and after five years of marriage to me she fell in love with a Brazilian statesman and divorced me to marry him." He placed a hand over his heart, and with feigned melodrama proclaimed, "And so, I've been a lonely, wandering bachelor for nearly twelve years."

"Whatever," Delilah said sardonically.

Changing the subject, Eli suggested that Delilah go with him to Arkansas the following week. He pointed out that not only did she need to meet the ranchers that she would be doing business with, but she also needed to learn the artificial insemination process. This took Delilah by surprise.

"You mean they don't," she began, but then she caught herself. "I thought they just . . . you know."

Eli's eyebrows shot up and he smiled. "Just . . . what?"

"Okay, so it's artificial insemination," she finally said. "Interesting."

Eli went on to explain that because any thoroughbred foal resulting from or produced by the process of Artificial Insemination is not eligible for registration, one of the ranchers, Cletus Clovis was bringing his prized mare for breeding the old fashioned way. The other rancher, Bart Webster, was more interested in quantity than quality, and would be using the artificial insemination process.

"Cletus owned the horse that sired Henry's Last Hoorah," Eli told her. "The name of that horse was Henry's Got Bank. He died shortly after impregnating Nettie's mare." He chuckled. "That's how Nettie, ever the smart ass, came up with the name Henry's Last Hoorah."

Delilah laughed.

The following morning after breakfast, Delilah told Eli she would give the trip to

Arkansas careful consideration. She explained that any hesitation was born out of the threats she'd received against her and the ranch. To further her concern, she feared for Gus's safety. Her ringing cell phone interrupted Eli's attempts to put her mind at ease.

"Guess what?" Dooby said excitedly the second Delilah answered the phone. "Raven Wood's for sale, and I bought it."

There was a deafening silence as Delilah processed what she'd just heard. "NO WAY!" she finally replied.

Dooby shared the particulars with Delilah as Eli listened with curiosity to Delilah's side of the conversation. And when the call was concluded she shook her head with amused astonishment.

"He always said that one day he'd own it, and now he does," she said with a chuckle. "Nothing could ever induce me to buy Raven Wood; family connection or not."

She looked at Eli who was wearing a tremendous question mark on his face and realized her inner monologue had just become public. "The place is haunted!" she qualified.

"What are you talking about?" Eli asked.

"One of the largest plantations in Georgia, built in the early nineteenth century by J. P. Raven," Delilah began. "Well, it used to be one of the largest. Most of the land was sold off decades ago. The house and twenty acres is all that's left of the original property. That is to say, most of the original house remains. There were a number of fires over the years, and countless owners who attempted restoration. But no one stayed long enough to complete the restorations. It's been abandoned for nearly fifty years now."

"What makes you think it's haunted?" Eli asked.

"I've only been there once," Delilah said with a shiver. "And it only took once for me to believe it was haunted, and to know that I'd never step foot there again.

"I had heard about Raven Wood all my life. Everyone talked about it. Everyone had their own story to tell. Dooby had a slight obsession with the place because his ancestors had been slaves there.

"Legend has it that J. P. Raven left the property to his only son, Patrick, who, unlike his father, was one of the cruelest, most wicked men in Georgian history. He supposedly murdered his first wife, though it could never be proven, and drove his second wife, and mother of his four children, insane. Poor thing, she spent the last eight years of her life locked in the attic. His two sons fought on opposite sides in the civil war, and never made it home. One daughter, Aribelle, abandoned the family and Raven Wood altogether, while the other daughter, youngest of the four, stayed at home to take care of her mother, father and the plantation. The mother died, and shortly after, the daughter had a mysterious accident and died, too."

Eli shook his head. "Tragic," he said.

"Yes, well the tragedy doesn't end there," Delilah continued, as she made her way to the living room and plopped down on the sofa. "Aribelle's son inherited the place and was met with one catastrophe after another until he sold it and moved on. There's a story of a couple carpenters who had been hired to renovate the place in the early nineteen hundreds. Evidently they were so frightened they walked, or ran, from the job and didn't even bother to take their tools with them. They would never tell what happened and would turn ashen at the mere mention of Raven Wood. Most of the owners would leave within a year of moving in, and those few who stayed longer, met with untimely, macabre ends."

"And these bizarre events don't dissuade Dooby from owning it?" Eli asked, as he joined Delilah on the sofa.

"You would think so, wouldn't you?" Delilah said. "But Dooby has a different mindset than most. I suppose being raised by a psychic has something to do with that."

Once again, Eli looked puzzled.

"Dooby's mother is a psychic," Delilah said. "One of the best in Georgia. Though, I have to say, she's rather put off by Raven Wood, too. I wonder what she thinks about Dooby owning it."

"You liked the house, didn't you?" Eli said. "Even though it frightened you."

"I loved the house," she answered. "That's just it. I'm certain others had, HAVE the same reaction. I know this sounds absolutely ludicrous, but it's almost like the house . . . casts a spell on people. It's as though the house never belongs to anyone, but they belong to the house. And that's the problem. You become so overwhelmed by . . . adoration for the structure that you just abandon all good judgment.

"Being there is like being in your own, personal horror movie," she said. "I've always said I'd be the first girl to die in a horror movie. You know, running through the woods with an ax murderer hot on my heels, wearing nothing but an oversized man's shirt and one four-inch stiletto, while waving the other shoe in my hand and screaming like a little girl."

Eli laughed heartily. "I'm not a big fan of horror movies, but I'd pay money to see that one."

Their eyes met and held a long moment. He placed the back of his hand softly against Delilah's cheek and slowly leaned into her.

Chapter 6

Mordecai Pulapup

Delilah's heart pounded, and she felt flush as Eli's hand crept to the top of her head and then back down again in a balled fist.

"There was a bug in your hair," he said as he opened his hand to reveal a creepy crawly.

Delilah shot off the sofa with a shrill scream and began jumping about; slapping at her long black curls with both hands.

Gus, the toothless ranch hand, came bounding into the room accompanied by the Lincoln County Sherriff, who had drawn his gun.

"What'th going on in here?" Gus said forcefully.

"A bug in her hair," Eli said, suppressing a grin, and rising from the sofa.

The sheriff holstered his weapon, and gave Eli a curt nod. "Eli," he said.

"Sheriff," Eli replied with a measure of animosity that did not go unnoticed by Delilah, who was attempting to put her mussed hair and clothing right.

"When did YOU get back?" the sheriff asked Eli.

"Couple days ago," Eli offered.

"How long you staying?" the sheriff prodded.

Eli looked at Delilah, then at Gus, and then back to the sheriff. A smile inched across Eli's face. "Longer than usual," he said.

The sheriff's eyes narrowed slightly, and it was clear to everyone in the room that he didn't know how to respond to the answer. Or, at the very least, he was weighing the consequences of his response. The tension between the two men grew perceptibly thicker.

Attempting to break the strain, Delilah said, in her sweetest, long southern drawl, "what can I do for you sheriff?"

"I promised Dooby I'd check on you," he said, as he looked suspiciously at Eli. "Is everything alright?"

"Fine," Delilah said. Sensing doubt, she added, "trust me, you'll be the first one I call if something happens."

The Sheriff excused himself and was escorted to the back door by Gus.

"What's going on between the two of you?" Delilah demanded of Eli.

"Later," Eli responded, as he bolted from the room.

Delilah ran to the kitchen, peered through the window over the sink, and watched Eli chase after the sheriff. The two men stood beside the sheriff's patrol car, engaged in a short conversation. When Eli returned to the house Delilah continued her interrogation.

"What was that all about?" she asked.

"I told him you were going to Arkansas with me next week for a few days. He's going to check in with Gus while we're gone," Eli replied.

"I don't recall actually deciding to go to Arkansas, much less sharing that decision with you," Delilah said with a hint of rebellion.

Eli flashed a flirtatious grin, lightly pinched Delilah's chin, and with a mischievous glint in his green eyes said, "you're going."

In a span of about three seconds Delilah's mind was engaged in a battle. Was Eli being obnoxiously assertive or simply decisive? She could be irritated that a man she barely knew, who had suddenly reappeared from her distant past, was making decisions concerning her life without consulting her first, or she could be impressed with his confidence. At the same time, she couldn't help but be exceedingly curious about the exchange between Eli and the sheriff. She decided to Scarlett the former, concluding that it was much too complicated and needed further evaluation. Curiosity won out.

"Are you going to tell me what's going on between you and the sheriff?" Delilah asked.

"No," Eli replied as he snatched a set of keys from the peg board by the back door. "I'm taking the truck to town. Do you need anything?"

"Cushing or Stroud?" she inquired.

"Cushing," he replied.

"Can you stop by Naifeh's and get a couple pints of tabouli?"

"Sure," Eli said as he went out the door.

Perplexed, Delilah stood at the back door shaking her head while she watched Eli climb into the pickup. "What just happened here?" she thought out loud.

Delilah was cleaning the stalls in the barn when Eli returned. At the sound of the truck horn she put away the pitch fork and headed toward the house. As she came upon the truck she couldn't help but notice a full load of iron and various other metals in different shapes and sizes in the back of the truck. She looked up to see Eli coming out the back door of the house.

"What's all this?" Delilah asked the minute Eli was in ear shot.

"It's the new security gate I'm installing at the end of the drive," he replied nonchalantly. "Or it will be as soon as I've built it."

"Ith that the material for the gate?" Gus asked as he walked up behind Delilah.

"Yeah," Eli replied. "You want to help me unload it? It would be safer to do the welding here on the concrete. It's too dry down at the barn."

Delilah held her tongue. She proceeded to the house where she began preparing supper. The closer the pot of water came to boiling, the closer she came to boiling. By the time Gus and Eli came through the back door, Delilah was ready to throw a pot or two at Eli.

The men washed their hands and sat down at the table. Without a word, Delilah sat their plates down in front of them. She filled her plate, and placed it on the table.

"We have to talk," Delilah said ominously.

Gus's eyes went wide, and Eli put down the fork full of fettuccini that had been half way to his mouth.

"I don't want to come off as ungrateful," Delilah began calmly and rationally, but as she continued, calm gave way to a bit of a tirade. "But you have GOT to start consulting me with matters that concern me or this ranch. I never agreed to go to Arkansas and I wouldn't have approved of the expense of a security gate!"

"I told you I was paying for the gate," Eli said.

"No," Delilah said. "You never said anything to me about the gate."

Eli's expression was truly one of shock. He looked at Gus for confirmation. "Didn't we talk about this?" he asked.

"WE talked about it, but Delilah wathn't there at the time," Gus answered.

Eli burst into raucous laughter which was joined shortly thereafter by Gus's raucous laughter. But when the two men finally realized that Delilah wasn't nearly as amused as they were, the room became silent. Gus hung his head, and Eli looked like a little boy about to be scolded.

"I'm sorry, Delilah," Eli said beseechingly. "Honestly, I thought we talked about it. Don't worry about the money. I've got it covered. A security gate is long overdue. I tried several times to convince Nettie to have one installed."

"Obviously that didn't work," Delilah said, softening to Eli's sincerity. She smiled at the thought of Aunt Nettie. "How did she talk you out of it?"

"Well, Nettie had a way of making a point or getting someone's attention," Eli said.

Gus laughed. "Yeah. You can earn a lot of rethpect with the click clack of a ninety-theven Winchethter Riot shot gun."

"Or the hammer being cocked on her Sheriff's Colt .45," Eli offered. "Not that she ever pulled a gun on me. But I did witness that move a time or two. Did you ever know ole Pete Jenkins, Gus?"

Delilah cleared her throat.

With that, Eli promised to be more conscientious about Delilah's involvement in ranch matters, and vowed never to speak on her behalf without her consent; mortal peril being the only exclusion to the promise. Delilah was satisfied.

By the end of the week the gate had been constructed. And on Saturday evening, as Delilah left for her poker game, Eli and Gus were installing it at the end of the drive. Eli advised her that it would be Monday before the control unit would be wired, and he would leave the gate open for her that evening.

Delilah followed the directions given to her by Karon, and found the house with ease. Once on the porch, she rang the door bell. She could hear chatter inside but no one came to the door so she rang the bell again. After a bit, Karon threw the door open.

"Girl, what are you doin' out on the porch?" Karon asked.

"Waiting for someone to answer the door bell," Delilah said as she stepped through the door and gave Karon a hug.

"Oh, that's what that sound was," Karon said. "No one ever knocks or rings the bell at my house. You just walk on in."

Delilah took a seat at the kitchen table as Karon made the introductions to a classy, well dressed, older woman, in her early to mid-sixties, named Patty, Patty's grand-daughter, Sophie, a curvy young lady with long red hair, and piercing blue, almond shaped eyes, and last but not least, Odie, a voluptuous, raven haired woman with dark saucer shaped eyes, in her forties.

After the introductions the ladies ate, and once the dishes were cleared from the table, the first hand of poker was dealt.

An hour later, Delilah had learned that the brooding Sophie was an aspiring screenplay writer who lived a privileged life in Oklahoma City with her Daddy Warbucks type husband,

Carl. And the quick witted Odie, who bought and sold antiques on the internet, lived in Cushing with her carpenter husband, Diesel. While these insights were amusing, they were nothing in comparison to the revelation about the widow Patty, who had not only known Aunt Nettie and been friends with her, but had actually been present at the infamous poker game that resulted in Nettie winning The Royal Flush Ranch.

Upon discovering that Delilah was Nettie's niece, Patty regaled the gathering with a blow by blow account of Nettie's acquisition.

"I thought you looked familiar," Patty said excitedly. "I've seen pictures of you when I visited Nettie at the ranch. She was sharp as a tack, your aunt," Patty finally concluded as she shuffled the cards and then began dealing. "Texas Hold 'em, Ladies. Does everyone have their nickel in the pot?"

As the poker games continued, the relationship dots were connected between Delilah, Dooby, and Karon. At Karon's insistence, Delilah told the story of how she and Dooby become lifelong friends.

The corners of Delilah's mouth turned up slightly. "Our dads go fishing together all the time, and when we were children they would often times take us with them. Dooby was always instructed to look out for me and it was pretty obvious he resented playing babysitter.

"Well, on one of our fishing expeditions, after thirty minutes or so of pouting and mumbling about watching the silly little white girl, I decided to relieve Dooby of his burden and walk back to town. Now mind you, I was five years old and he was six. I just felt so sorry for him. He wanted to fish with the men, and instead he had to tend to my every whim.

"To this day no one is certain how we got separated from the adults, or how I managed to slip away unnoticed. But it happened.

"So, after I'd walked a quarter mile, or so, I got tired and decided to rest a little in a thicket of trees off the side of the road. I fell asleep.

"A couple hours later a man and woman found me, and took me to the bait shop where a command post had been set up. Evidently a good number of the community and law enforcement had been looking for me. And dive teams had been called in to search the lake."

A collective gasp sounded around the table.

"Well, by the time we got to the bait shop a mob had formed. They were on the verge of attacking Dooby; one bigoted old man in particular who was accusing Dooby of 'doing something to me.' I grasped Dooby's hand and told them it wasn't Dooby's fault; that I had left so Dooby could fish.

"And then, all I remember is the old man lunging for Dooby like he was going to choke him or something, and I sort of jumped between the two, and then the man pushed me out of the way. I guess he didn't realize how much force he'd used because he knocked me into a large metal pop box.

"When I woke up several hours later in the hospital, Dooby was sitting beside me, holding my hand. I could tell he'd been crying. He just looked at me and said, 'I'll never let them hurt you again.'

"His mother told him that I was sent here to be his baby sister," Delilah added. "She said that it didn't matter that our skin was different, or that we had different parents. And then she told him that big brothers always take care of their little sisters. And he's been doing just that ever since."

Four pairs of eyes glistened in the silence.

"Is that the story he told you?" Delilah asked Karon.

"Yeah, pretty much," Karon said with a sniffle. "And I have to confess I was a little suspicious of your relationship with him until I heard it. I just found it hard to believe a man could care that much for a woman he wasn't . . . you know."

"Sleeping with?" Patty said.

"Well, yeah," Karon admitted.

"Let's play poker," Sophie said. And she dealt a hand of five card draw.

"What do you do?" Odie asked Delilah.

"Well, I was an interior designer," Delilah began. "I owned a shop in Macon, but had to sell it after the death of my fourth husband."

Another thunderous silence fell at the table. Delilah took a deep breath and conveyed the story of her five husbands and their strange and untimely deaths.

Sophie smiled for the first time that evening, and explained that Delilah's life story could quite possibly be her next project. She then intimated that the project she was currently working on was a heavy, melancholy drama, and, that it was greatly affecting her mood.

The poker game concluded and the ladies agreed to meet two weeks later at Delilah's. Telephone numbers were exchanged as well as hugs all around. Delilah was delighted at the prospect of having a few females in her life to balance out the male influence. She found that the older she got, the more difficult it was to form new friendships. The older she got, the more history there was to share, and typically it was exhausting to share it. But tonight it hadn't been exhausting. She had left the party with an odd sense of contentment and peace.

That is until she arrived to her dark and seemingly abandoned home, and a sinking feeling in her stomach replaced the peace. As she pulled the pickup next to the garage, the feeling sank even further when she saw a note attached to Pandora's vacant pen. She jumped from the pickup and dashed to the pen. She wrenched the note free and read, *I never liked that goat!*

"Oh no!" Delilah cried. Her eyes filled with tears, and her heart raced as she scanned the perimeter for any sign of Pandora, or worse, (the thought now occurred to her) Mr. Creepy, who could possibly be lurking about in the shadows.

In a matter of seconds she saw the lights and heard the distinct sound of Gus's truck at the end of the drive.

Before Eli could exit the truck, Delilah was waving the note at him and sobbing. "He's killed my goat! He's KILLED my goat! She was an innocent animal. Why would anyone want to harm an innocent animal?"

Once out of the truck, an alarmed Eli took the note from Delilah and read it while Gus made his way to stand by Delilah.

With a scowl, Eli glanced quickly at the house, then at the barn, and then at Delilah and Gus.

"You two stay here," Eli said. "I'm going to check out the house."

Ignoring Eli's request to stay outside, Delilah followed him in the back door, through the kitchen, and quietly down the hall.

"Do you hear that?" Delilah whispered, referencing the thumping and scratching sound coming from upstairs.

"Yeah," Eli said in a low voice as he tiptoed into the living room and retrieved Nettie's .45 Ruger from the gun cabinet. He released the clip to make sure it was loaded, and then as gently as possible inserted it back into the gun.

"You stay down here," he adamantly mouthed to Delilah, and then he trekked up the stairs. A few seconds later he shouted over the upstairs banister. "Delilah, I think you better come up here."

When Delilah reached her bedroom door it looked like a twister had swept through the room. Her eight foot Ficus tree lay on its side, removed from its pot. Small pieces of furniture and lamps had been turned over. Bottles of perfume, jewelry, and pictures were strewn about. And lying on top of her bed, amongst a cloud of goose down feathers, in the middle of a shredded comforter, was Pandora the goat, who was eating Delilah's best silk night gown.

"I'm going to kill that goat!" Delilah said.

At the sound of Delilah's voice, Pandora became aware that she wasn't the only one in the room. She bounded from the bed and headed straight for Delilah, where she began gently butting Delilah with her head and rubbing against her like a cat.

Eli laughed. "Not ten minutes ago you were hysterical because you thought someone had harmed her."

"That's different," Delilah said, suppressing a smile as she scratched Pandora's head. "Ten minutes ago she was a helpless, innocent creature. Now she's a destructive, maniacal goat who's trashed my room and eaten my favorite nighty."

Eli tucked the gun in the waist band of his jeans, and escorted Pandora down the stairs and out the back door. Once the animal was back in her pen, Eli and Gus searched the other buildings on the premises while Delilah cleaned up Pandora's mess.

The following morning after breakfast, Delilah called the sheriff to add another complaint of trespassing to the ever growing list of complaints against her mystery stalker. The sheriff made his notes, and sensing Delilah's consternation, he attempted to add a little levity by asking her if she wanted to press charges against Pandora for destruction of private property. Delilah chuckled, and then ended the call.

Monday rolled around, and the security system was installed at the gate. Delilah packed for her trip to Arkansas with Eli, and prepared the house, including several meals, for Gus's stay. She had hesitantly agreed to make the trip as long as Gus camped out in the big house.

Delilah and Eli departed from the ranch early Tuesday morning with the prized stud horse, Henry's Last Hoorah, secured in the trailer behind them.

Their five hour drive to Conway was filled with light and pleasant conversation, sprinkled with an occasional laugh. The spark of attraction Delilah had originally felt for Eli was compounded by an ever growing fondness for him, which was not met kindly with her voice of resistance.

"Almost there," Eli said as they exited the freeway north onto Highway 25, "I should warn you about the Webster clan. Bart, the owner of the ranch, and Caroline, his wife, are normal enough, but . . . "

Eli went on to say that one of their sons had turned survivalist and was now living off the land and apparently wrestling bears somewhere in Colorado. Their other son was a brilliant but extraordinarily eccentric artist in New York City, and their daughter, Morda Kay, was a flirtatious, blonde beauty who loved falling in love but didn't care much for the tedium of normal, everyday relationships, which resulted in several marriages, none of which lasted more than a year. When Delilah pointed out that SHE had been married five times, Eli reminded Delilah that her marriages didn't end out of boredom.

The obvious question was dancing on the tip of Delilah's tongue. Did Eli ever have a relationship with her; fleeting or otherwise? He had given her very little to go on. Opting to Scarlett that thought, Delilah went in another direction.

"Morda Kay?" Delilah questioned. "That's an unusual name."

"She was named after Caroline's father, Mordecai Pulapup," Eli said with a grin. "The other wild card. He was the original owner of the ranch, and gave it to Bart & Caroline. He lives with them. He's just a few days shy of ancient, can't hear thunder, and carries a cane which he frequently uses for more than a walking stick."

The inquisitive look on Delilah's face prompted Eli to add, "I'll just let you see for yourself."

They arrived at the Pulapup Hill Ranch with its massive iron gated entrance. Their long, winding drive through the property took them past a sizeable, rock gate house, followed by a large, rock boat house that sat on the edge of a small lake, then the stables and bunk house the size of Wal-Mart, and finally to the hotel size, rock mansion at the end of the mile long drive.

Delilah gasped. "Well," she said, "I guess I'll stop feeling guilty for charging such exorbitant stud fees."

Eli shot a furtive glance at Delilah and chuckled softly.

The two were met at the front door by Bart and Caroline. Introductions were made while a thin Hispanic man and a plump Hispanic woman gathered the over-night bags from the pickup. Caroline quickly gave them instructions as to which bedrooms in the south wing to place the baggage.

The welcoming continued as the party entered the capacious foyer through double oak doors. Quite suddenly there was a thunderous banging coming from a room off the foyer, and a raspy masculine voice shouted, "what the hell's goin' on in there?"

At the same moment a tall, thin, blonde beauty in tight blue jeans, clinging knit top, and four inch stilettos, came bounding down the stairs singing Eli's name. By the time she reached Eli and threw her arms around his neck, Mordecai had shuffled into the room.

Mordecai was the picture-perfect old geezer. The waistband of his trousers was "suspendered" a good distance above his waist, though it was difficult to tell exactly where his waist was because he was hunkered over; supported by his cane. The two remaining hairs on the right side of his head were meticulously swept over to the left ear, and his perfect, porcelain, portable dentures clicked like castanets.

"It's Eli, Grandpa!" Morda Kay squealed, as she clung tighter to Eli's neck, and then she kissed his cheek.

"Well don't that beat all," Mordecai yelled, pulling his grand-daughter away from Eli, and shaking Eli's hand. "This your wife?" he added with a nod toward Delilah.

With a raised voice, Eli introduced Nettie Mae's niece to Mordecai.

"What do ya mean next May's knees?" Mordecai questioned. "Who is this pretty little thing you brought with you?"

Once Mordecai understood who Delilah was, and he reminisced about Nettie, Delilah and Eli excused themselves and spent the afternoon at the stables going over the artificial insemination process. They returned to the mansion at 5:00 to clean-up for supper promptly at 7:00.

Delilah dressed in her little black, sleeveless dress with a plunging neck line and soft flowing skirt. She slipped on her high heels, applied lipstick one more time, and fluffed her long black curls. She looked at herself in the mirror. She had never had a thin, willowy stature like Morda Kay, nor had she ever wished it. She was perfectly content with her five-foot, eight-inch, curvalicious figure. And even though the past twenty years had added a bit more sand to her hour glass figure, the sand had been evenly distributed.

Delilah took hold of the banister and started her descent down the opulent staircase. Eli stood about ten feet from the base of the stairs, engaged in a spirited conversation with Caroline and Morda Kay. He shot a fleeting glance toward Delilah, but then lingered much longer on the double take. As she reached the bottom stair, Eli stepped toward her, holding out his hand.

"You look lovely," he whispered in her ear.

"You don't think it's too much cleavage, do you?" Delilah fretted in a low voice.

Eli grinned. "Uh . . . no."

"Love your shoes," Morda Kay interrupted, pointing at Delilah's feet. "Last season Jimmy Choos, if I'm not mistaken."

"Oh," Delilah replied with surprise. "Thank you. They were a Christmas gift from my mother. I actually asked for a double-bevel, compound miter saw."

"Well, you can't wear a saw," Morda Kay said snidely.

"That's exactly what my mother said," Delilah retorted pleasantly. "But you can't build things with an open-toed sling-back."

"You got a string on your back?" Mordecai asked as he entered the room with a tap of his cane, and a shuffle of his slipper covered feet. He reached toward Delilah's back. "Let me get that for ya."

Finding no string, Mordecai announced that someone must have already removed it, and the party made their way into the dining room.

"You're 'bout the purdiest thing I ever seen," Mordecai shouted to Delilah as he struggled to pull out her chair. "Sure don't take after your Aunt Nettie. Right plain woman, Nettie was. But I reckon she couldn't be matched in spirit."

"Thanks, Sir," Delilah said with a smile.

"No, I ain't a banker," Mordecai replied. "I'm a rancher. Least I WAS back in the day. And let me tell you, back in the day I woulda moved heaven and earth to court you. Just couldn't resist a woman with blue eyes and wide hips."

"Daddy!" Caroline exclaimed.

"Now, Sister," Mordecai said to his daughter. "This purdy little thing knows a compliment when she hears one, don't ya?"

Dinner was a feast of comedies with large helpings of Mordecai's misinterpretations of conversations, seasoned with the rapping of his cane on the table when he finally understood, several courses of Eli deflecting the hand Morda

Kay had placed on his thigh, and the sweet dessert of amusement Delilah indulged in at Eli's struggle to ignore the ever persistent sexual innuendo and double-entendre's supplied by the blonde beauty.

"No brandy, Daddy," Caroline scolded, after the party had adjourned to the living room.

"It's a right sad day when a man can't even have a brandy after supper," Mordecai complained.

"I think I'll take a walk down by the lake," Morda Kay simpered. "Why don't you join me, Eli?"

"I'm exhausted," he replied. "Been a long day, and lots to do tomorrow. Think I'll just turn in."

Bart, Caroline, and Delilah agreed that the hour was late. Everyone trudged up the stairs and to their rooms. Eli stopped Delilah outside her bedroom door.

"I'm in the room at the end of the hall if you need anything," Eli said.

"Thanks," Delilah said. "I'm sure I'll be fine."

A moment of silence stretched between them in which each studied the other. Delilah was unsure if Eli was waiting for an invitation from her, or perhaps mustering the courage to invite her to join him. She felt her cheeks flush with anticipation. Eli reached out and took hold of her arm, and Delilah caught her breath.

"Well, goodnight Delilah," he said. And then he kissed her cheek.

She bid him goodnight, and went in her room. After changing into night clothes, washing her face, and tidying her room, she crawled between the cool silk sheets. She reached for the table lamp, and with a little click, extinguished the light from the room. Within a few minutes she was hovering in that place just between consciousness and deep, blissful sleep. She heard something that sounded like a door opening. Dream? Time seemed immeasurable, and images began to flash. The covers were being pulled gently, and the bed was moving. The face of her second husband popped in her mind, then the face of her first husband, then Eli's face.

Her eyes went wide and she gasped, as she realized this was no dream. With a shriek, Delilah bolted from the bed, covers in hand and held to her chin, causing her uninvited guest to roll off the other side of the bed and land with a thud on the floor. There was a brief moment of silence, followed by a low groan, and then a symphony of colorful expletives.

Chapter 7

Cletus Clovis

Slowly but surely, Mordecai sat up and locked eyes with Delilah.

"Young Lady, what the devil are you doin' in my room?" he yelled.

Delilah remained fixed on the other side of the bed, covers held tightly to her chin. "I beg your pardon, Sir," she shouted as she reached to turn on the lamp. "I thought this was my room."

A squinty-eyed Mordecai looked around the room. "Well, don't that beat all. I guess this IS your room," he said as he began the daunting task of getting to his feet.

As Delilah dropped the covers and started toward the other side of the bed to render some assistance, Eli came bolting through the door wearing nothing but pajama bottoms.

"Delilah?" he said upon entering the room. And then he realized she was not alone. "Mordecai?"

"It ain't what you think, son," Mordecai said as Delilah hoisted him to his feet.

"Daddy!" Caroline exclaimed from the door way. She and Bart rushed into the room, and seized the old man's arm. "You've been in the brandy again, haven't you?" She sniffed at his shoulder. "And a cigar, too? Daddy!"

As it turned out, this had not been the first time old Mordecai had slipped back downstairs for a nip after changing into his pajamas, and then returned to a room that wasn't his. After a flood of apologies to Delilah, Caroline told the story of one instance where he'd climbed into bed with Bart's aunt, and neither realized the error until the following morning. Or at least, that was the story he was sticking to.

After dressing in blue jeans, work boots, and T-shirt the following morning, Delilah pulled her long, black curls into a ponytail, applied a light layer of mascara to her eye lashes and a dab of lip gloss to her lips. She then proceeded downstairs to the dining room where a breakfast fit for a king had been spread out on a massive sideboard.

Delilah was alone in the dining room and hesitated filling her plate until she was joined by the others. But she didn't know where the others were. Only a few moments passed, however, before she was joined by Morda Kay, who flitted into the room wearing skinny jeans, a low cut V-neck T-shirt, and alligator boots.

"Good morning, Delilah," she said enthusiastically. "Where's Eli?"

"And good morning to you, Morda Kay," Delilah replied with equal enthusiasm. "I have no idea where Eli is."

"Well, he's not in his room," Morda Kay said as she sauntered over to the buffet and began filling a plate. "Were you going to have breakfast?"

"Well, yes," Delilah said, slightly confused. "I was just waiting for the others."

"Oh, we don't wait breakfast around here."

Delilah nodded and fell in behind Morda Kay, filling her own plate. The two women took their seats at the table; one on one side, one on the other, and began eating.

"Delilah, can I ask you a personal question?" Morda Kay said after a bit. "Are you and Eli . . . you know . . . involved?"

After swallowing a mouth full of eggs and dabbing the corners of her mouth with her napkin, Delilah replied with a smile, "no."

This seemed the exact response the perky, blonde was hoping for. "I just wondered," she said. "I mean, I could totally understand if you were interested in him. He's just so . . . dreamy. I've always had a thing for the Matthew McConaughey types."

Delilah puzzled over this statement a moment. She had never given it much thought. But now that it was brought to mind she could see a slight resemblance; the twisted, mischievous grin that could stretch into a full blown 1000 watt smile, the flirtatious glint in the eyes, and of course, their coloring and build were similar.

Eli entered the dining room as if called upon by the power of suggestion, followed shortly thereafter by Mordecai and Caroline. While preparing her father's breakfast plate, Caroline continued with apologies for the previous night's escapade until Delilah assured her that the look of surprise on Mordecai's face was sufficient evidence of his innocence. In a gesture of good will, Delilah hugged the old man's neck, kissed his cheek, and jokingly advised him he'd be wearing a lamp if he tried it again. Mordecai laughed heartily, rapped his cane on the table, and told her she was a good girl.

After hurriedly consuming his breakfast, and gulping down a cup of coffee, Eli pushed away from the table and stood with his hands in his jean's pockets. "Well," he said, as he stepped toward the dining room door. "Thank you for breakfast, Caroline. Don't count on us for lunch. Delilah, let's go. We don't want to keep Mr. Clovis waiting."

Caroline scowled and exhaled a long breath of disgust. "Did you tell her about Cletus?"

"No," Eli replied. "Didn't want to scare her off."

The only thing Delilah knew about Cletus Clovis was his name, that he was one of the two ranchers paying for Henry's Last Hoorah's little swimmers, and that he'd owned the horse that sired her horse.

In wide-eyed horror Delilah looked from Eli to Caroline. "What?" she begged.

"Delilah," Caroline said. "The man's an ill-tempered, misogynistic pig. He can smell fear a mile away and he'll capitalize on it. The best advice I can give you is to stand your ground, and DON'T let him intimidate you."

"You're awfully quiet," Eli observed as they drove toward the stables. "Don't be afraid of Cletus."

"I'm not," Delilah said confidently. "I've encountered nasty dispositions before, and I'll encounter them again. Still, it's good to have a little warning. It gives me the opportunity to put on my game face and emotional armor."

Eli smiled and nodded approvingly. "I can't deny Cletus has his faults, but he's also one of the best, if not THE best horseman in the country. You can learn a lot from him."

They arrived at the colossal stable, and Eli pulled into one of the nine bays. They exited the truck and walked the short distance to the group of men gathered around Henry's Last Hoorah.

"Eli," Bart called out when he saw the pair.

A large man with shoulder length, wavy grey hair, cold, dark eyes, and a serious scowl turned to face Eli and Delilah.

"'Bout time," the man said with a deep, rough voice. "Eli," he said, extending his hand toward Eli.

Eli stepped forward and shook Cletus' hand. "Good to see you, Cletus."

Cletus looked at Delilah. "They tell me you're Nettie's niece," he said as the creases in his brow deepened.

"Yes, Sir," she said with a warm smile, extending her hand to shake his. "Delilah Beauregard, Sir."

"Humph," Cletus grunted, and then he turned his back on Delilah.

And so the tone was set for the rest of the day. Delilah was pleasantly observant and quiet until she had a question which was generally answered by the equine authority with condescension and, on occasion, condemnation.

Praise was freely given to Eli for the excellent condition of Henry, only to be completely ignored when Eli made it clear that the horse's condition was to Delilah's credit.

Throughout the day, while giving instructions, Cletus would sarcastically interject that it was much easier to throw a recipe together, or hang clothes out on the line to dry, or change a baby's diaper, than it was to run a ranch. Delilah wondered just how many diaper's Cletus had changed in his lifetime. She was betting on zero.

It was true; she had encountered nasty dispositions in her time. But Cletus Clovis took the prize for the nastiest.

By day's end, Delilah had endured all she could. Her tank of charm and kindness was empty. Now it was time for force. With the last insult she threw back her shoulders, and lifted her head with determination. "Mr. Clovis, may I ask you a personal question?" Giving the man no time to answer, she steamed forward. "Is your hatred of women a result of how you were nurtured, or is it just in your nature?"

The entire place went silent. The wide-eyed ranch hands exchanged worried glances with Bart and Eli. Henry's Last Hoorah neighed gently, and bobbed his head.

"You're quite the little sass, aren't you?" Cletus sneered.

"No sass intended, Sir. This is purely curiosity; a desire to understand you better." Delilah trudged on. "You see, the answer to that question will determine how I feel about you. If you were raised that way, then I'm inclined to pity you for not knowing better, and pity you for not having the impetus to learn and change. If it's just in your nature, then I'm free to despise you. In any case, be assured I'll pray for you. And, either way, it's certain I'll take the appropriate action to NEVER be in your company again."

Cletus's face became beet red with anger, and his eyes filled with rage. His hand balled into a fist, and he raised it as he took a step toward Delilah.

In an instant, Eli took hold of Delilah and turned her away from Cletus. Bart stepped in front of Cletus, and took him by the arms. "Now, come on Cletus. No need for that."

Eli escorted Delilah to the coral outside of the stables, and they sat on the edge of a trough.

"I'm sorry," Delilah said. "That was stupid. I'd just taken all I could take. Behavior like that is totally unacceptable."

"I think your behavior was justified," Eli said, placing an arm around Delilah.

Delilah pulled away from Eli and glared at him. "I was talking about HIS behavior. And for the record, I'm at a loss to understand why you, and the others, tolerate it. It makes you just as culpable as he, and perpetuates the maleficence."

A smile inched across Eli's face, and his green eyes sparkled with mischief. "I love the way you talk when you're angry," he said.

Delilah rolled her eyes and shook her head.

Cletus and Bart sauntered out of the stables, and Cletus asked to talk to Delilah, alone. Eli denied his request until Delilah assured him it was okay. Cletus took Eli's spot on the trough next to Delilah. Bart and Eli stepped away just out of ear shot, but still close enough to keep an eye on the two.

Cletus took a deep breath and sighed. "Nurture," he said softly. "I won't bore with details, but simply put, the women in my childhood were less than loving."

Delilah looked at him sympathetically and nodded. "And what about as an adult?" she asked softly.

"Not much different," he replied. He chuckled. "I tend to choose the wrong women."

"I heard a saying once," Delilah said with a smile. "'You keep doin' what you're doin' and you'll keep gettin' what you got.' Just food for thought. Have you ever had a GOOD female influence in your life?"

"One," Cletus replied. "Your aunt. It didn't take her long to draw a line in the sand. There was just something about her that convinced me I'd better not cross the line. She was a formidable woman; demanding respect, but in a respectful way." He laughed. "Something in her demeanor. Well, that plus the fact I'd been told she could shoot like a man." He paused a moment, then continued. "You remind me of her. You ain't a sharp shooter, are you?"

Delilah smiled as she quickly weighed her answer. "Well, I did shoot a man once."

Of course Delilah didn't mention that the man was Gus, her toothless ranch hand, or that she'd shot him accidently in the foot during her first and only encounter with a firearms. She felt there was no harm in allowing Cletus to believe she was an accomplished and potentially lethal markswoman.

"Look, I'm new at this ranching business," Delilah said. "But it doesn't take a seasoned rancher to know that you are a brilliant and gifted horseman. I'm in awe of your talents. But those talents are minimized by your ill-tempered attitude. I'd like nothing more than to be your friend; to learn all I can from you. But I simply can't allow you, or anyone else for that matter, to treat me the way you treated me today. What are your thoughts?"

Cletus chuckled. "Well, first, young lady, I owe you an apology. I'm sorry. Friends?" he said, extending his hand to be shaken.

"I hug my friends," Delilah said with a smile, and she threw an arm around his shoulders and squeezed.

The pair stood and walked toward a flabbergasted Eli and Bart. Cletus draped his arm around Delilah's shoulders. "You know, for a novice rancher you really are doing an excellent job with Henry," Cletus said.

"Well," Delilah said. "Since Gus taught me everything I know I'll be sure to pass the compliment on to him."

That evening, and for the first time in the long history of the ranchers' acquaintance, a remarkably jovial and frighteningly polite Cletus joined the others for dinner. Caroline's expression vacillated between an apprehensive smile and sheer amazement at Cletus's transformation. As the company made their way from the living room to the dining room, Caroline pulled Delilah aside and inquired as to what she had done to affect such a drastic change, to which Delilah replied, "just took your advice, Caroline."

Upon entering the dining room, Mordecai insisted on sitting next to Delilah, while Morda

Kay quickly maneuvered in next to Eli. As soon as Eli announced that he and Delilah would be leaving the next morning, Morda Kay began doubling her efforts to seduce Eli, who appeared to be amused by the spectacle.

"I take it you're not married," Mordecai yelled at Delilah after the dishes from the first course were removed from the table.

"No, Sir," Delilah replied. "I'm not."

"Surely you've been married," Mordecai continued. "Can't imagine a pretty little thing like you not having a husband."

"I've had FIVE husbands," Delilah said.

A hush fell at the table. And as was often the case, Delilah was met with looks of shock, confusion, and curiosity.

Delilah took a deep breath and prosaically recited the well practiced list. "My first husband was killed by a flying golf cart. My second husband was stung by a bee. My third husband fell into a vat of boiling chocolate. My fourth husband slipped in the shower and hit his head. And my fifth and last husband was shot by one of his two other wives."

After a long stretch of silence, Mordecai rapped his cane on the table leg, and burst out in laughter, shouting, "Damn, Honey, you're harder on husbands than Morda Kay!"

Morda Kay leaned into Eli and said in a whisper loud enough to be heard by all, "I'd stay away from that one if I were you."

Over the years Delilah had resolved to make light of her matrimonial misfortunes. It was that, or wallow in the sorrow of it. But on rare occasion, and most often when she least expected it, she was ambushed by the weight of her losses. This happened to be one of those occasions.

Though Delilah laughed heartily with the others to conceal her distress, she was actually overwhelmed momentarily with the urge to cry. She checked her emotions quickly, and looked around the table. She felt certain her morose moment had gone unnoticed by the others. That is until she caught sight of Eli, who had stopped laughing and looked at her with pained concern.

From that moment on, and for the remainder of the evening, Morda Kay could do nothing to entertain Eli, who kept a distant but watchful eye on Delilah. Eventually, the flirtatious blonde gave up her pursuits, and excused herself from the party with visible disappointment.

The following morning Eli and an unusually quiet Delilah departed from Pulapup Hill Ranch with Henry's Last Hoorah. Delilah sat reticent, looking out her window for the first thirty minutes of the journey. The further they went, the more concerned Eli became. He suspected the conversation about her husbands the previous evening was still weighing heavy on her mind, but he couldn't be certain.

He considered the question he wanted to ask; a question that had rarely produced positive results in the past. It was the question that opened the proverbial can of worms; the question that most men were taught at an early age never to ask.

"Do you want to talk about it?" he asked cautiously.

Delilah continued to stare out her window. "Talk about what?" she said with little emotion.

"Why you're so quiet," Eli answered.

Delilah shrugged and shook her head, still refusing to look in Eli's direction.

"Did I do or say something to hurt you?" Eli questioned.

"No!" Delilah exclaimed, turning quickly toward Eli. "No! Quite the contrary. You've been kind and . . . helpful, and . . . understanding." She shook her head. "It's not you."

"Does it bother you to talk about your husband's?" he asked.

"Most often not," she offered. "I've always known the choice of reactions is mine. And I choose not to get down about it. But on rare occasion sorrow has the upper hand, and ambushes me. Someone says something I'm not expecting, and I'm forced to surrender to the pain."

Eli nodded, and took in a deep breath. "You heard what Morda Kay said last night."

"Of course I heard. She intended for me to hear. I don't blame her."

Eli shot her a look of disbelief.

"No, I mean it," Delilah said adamantly. "I allowed her comment to vex me. I gave her permission. And to be perfectly honest . . . I was thinking the same thing about her!"

Eli laughed which prompted Delilah to smile. "I just didn't say it," she added defensively.

"I can't help but think of a Longfellow quote that Aunt Nettie was particularly fond of. 'If we could read the secret history of our enemies, we should find in each man's life sorrow and suffering enough . . .'"

"'To disarm all hostility,'" Eli finished.

"Yeah," Delilah said with a nod. "I wouldn't wish my secret history on anyone. Not even Morda Kay."

Delilah's tone turned serious again. "You realize she has a valid point. It's difficult, if not impossible, to deny that a serious involvement with me is a certain death sentence for men."

Eli shook his head vehemently. "No. I don't believe that."

Delilah chuckled. "You have that in common with my last three husbands."

The morbid conversation was mercifully interrupted by Delilah's ringing cell phone.

"Where are you?" Karon questioned adamantly, as soon as Delilah answered the call.

"Well, hello to you, too," Delilah fired back. "I'm in Arkansas, on my way home. Eli and I brought Henry's Last Hoorah to a rancher here. It's a long story, filled with intrigue, suspense, and zany characters."

"Mmm hmm. I'll bet," Karon said. "Speaking of zany characters, the girls want to play poker again, this weekend. You can tell me all about it then."

"That sounds wonderful," Delilah agreed. "Why don't y'all come to the ranch? Maybe I can talk Gus and Eli into joining us."

"Whateveh," Karon said. "I'll call everybody else and let them know. Seven sound good?"

"Seven it is," Delilah replied.

"By the way," Karon cautioned. "Dooby's tryin' to track you down."

Delilah's call waiting activated. "Yep," she said. "That's him. Got to go."

"So, you're in Arkansas," Dooby said at the first indication the call had connected.

"You called the house and talked to Gus, didn't you?" Delilah asked.

After getting a rundown of Delilah's activities, and giving Delilah an update on his renovation project in Macon, Dooby got to the point of his call.

"I had lunch with Big Daddy yesterday," Dooby began. "He's been keeping an ear to the ground for anything suspicious with Abigail, and he hasn't heard anything. I guess my ear's been on different ground because I have. I know a guy, who knows a guy, who's acquainted with a man who represents a wealthy socialite looking to 'eliminate' a woman in a mid-western state."

"That can't be good," Delilah said.

"The details are sketchy," Dooby continued. "So I can't be certain you're the target, or that Abigail's behind it. I just want to alert you to the possibility."

"Well, as you know, Abby's not the only one anxious for me to leave the ranch," Delilah reminded Dooby.

"I know," Dooby said. "And the sheriff is looking into things on your end. He's not ruling anyone out at this point. Listen, as soon as I finish up a few things here, I'm planning on coming back to Oklahoma."

"Dooby," Delilah urged. "You are always welcome, and I'd love to see you, but it's not necessary for you to come back. Take care of things there. You know I'll call if I need you."

"We'll see," Dooby said. "I'll talk to you soon. Love you."

"Love you, too." Delilah replied.

"See," Eli said. "Dooby's not dead."

"What?"

"You're very involved with Dooby, and he's still breathing."

"That's because Dooby is my brother, not my lover."

"Never?"

"No! Would you have sex with a sister?"

"No!"

The rest of the trip home was spent in speculative discussion about the two suspected of terrorizing Delilah. Though both concurred that the most likely culprit was Lunatic Murray, but they were far from ruling out Abigail The Deranged.

"She knows no boundaries when it comes to getting her way," Delilah informed Eli. "She took out a rival cheerleader in high school with rumor and propaganda. She blackmailed her husband's dad to get a marriage proposal from her husband. Then she had an affair with her husband's brother, and blackmailed him for fifty-one percent of his business, only to turn around and sell it."

"Damn!" Eli said. "Reminds me of someone I used to know."

"I don't think she's ever killed anyone, but I have no doubt she's capable if there's a profit in it," Delilah said.

As they approached the Stroud exit, Delilah felt a wave of warm, calm wash over her. And the instant they were heading north on Highway 99, the feeling intensified.

Eli slowed, and pulled into the drive. Stopping at the gate, he entered the pass code on the key pad, and the gate slowly slid to the right.

Delilah's eyes were fixed on the house perched at the top of the hill, peeking through the multitude of trunks, limbs, and budding leaves of the trees that stood between them. Until that moment, this had been Aunt Nettie's place, and Delilah simply the keeper. But as the truck crept up the winding drive and around the pond, it seemed to be whispering to Delilah, "welcome home." For the first time since her arrival on The Royal Flush Ranch months before, she felt like this WAS her true home; she was a part of it, and it, a part of her.

Gus came sauntering out the back door as Eli parked the truck in front of the garage. Delilah bolted from the passenger side and hastened toward Gus. She hugged his neck.

"It's good to be home," she said with a smile. "Did everything go alright? Where's Pandora? I didn't see her in the pen when we pulled up."

The words had no sooner been spoken, when the cantankerous goat came bounding up from behind Delilah, and knocked her feet out from under her.

The last thing Delilah remembered were Gus's arms reaching for her as she toppled over backward, and the back of her head forcefully making contact with some unknown object.

Chapter 8

Disappearing Act

"Delilah!" Eli said anxiously as he gently patted Delilah's cheeks. "Delilah? Wake up honey. Wake up."

"Should I call an ambulanth?" Gus asked nervously as he rubbed Delilah's hand.

Delilah's eyes blinked feverishly. "Ouch!" she exclaimed, reaching for the back of her head.

Eli drew in a deep breath, and sighed. "Let's get her in the house, Gus."

Gus and Eli hoisted Delilah to her feet, and then stood ready to catch her if she lost her balance. She swayed only marginally, but quickly steadied herself.

"Thanks," she said. "I think I'm good. Did you call me honey?"

Eli's eyes went wide. "No," he said.

Delilah looked from Eli to Gus, and back at Eli. "I thought . . . but I heard . . . never mind."

Aside from the goose egg on the back of Delilah's head from her unfortunate fall, she felt perfectly normal the next morning. Once out of bed, she showered, fixed her hair and makeup, slipped a sun dress over her head, and sandals on her feet. She went downstairs to the kitchen, where she prepared breakfast.

After breakfast, and a few household chores, she made a list of groceries and supplies, and headed to Cushing where she spent most of the day being incensed to the point of ire.

When she got home, late that afternoon, she unloaded the spoils of the day, and proceeded to the living room where she found Eli sitting in the easy chair with his bare feet propped up comfortably on the ottoman, reading the newspaper.

Delilah stood in the doorway a moment, glaring at the back side of the paper. She began waving her arms frantically above her head.

Eli gingerly folded the paper over. "What are you doing?" he asked.

"Can you see me?" Delilah asked, with her hands on her hips.

Now, as is often the case when a woman asks a man a question there is clearly no right answer for, Eli was a deer caught in headlights. His expression was blank at the onset, but quickly morphed into terror. His wide, jade green eyes moved rapidly from left to right, searching thin air for assistance, and then he proceeded with caution. "Uh . . . do you want me to see you?"

"I have been invisible all day," she began, agitated. "First, I stopped for lunch, waited for the hostess to seat me while she flitted back and forth, and then she seated two men who came in after me, who apparently didn't see me either. Then, some idiot turned in front of me at a traffic light. I left about thirty dollars of rubber at the intersection trying to stop. And then, AND THEN, some mindless Neanderthal at the grocery store pushes a shopping cart into the truck, with me standing right there, and walks away without a word of apology, OR effort to move the damn cart!"

Eli folded his paper, laid it on the table beside the chair, stood, and stepped toward Delilah. He kissed her cheek. "Yes, I see you," he said with a mischievous grin. "What did you get for dinner tonight?"

Delilah slapped his arm gently. "You are a master at consolation," she said sardonically. "You've made quite an art form of it. You'll have to teach me how to do that, one of these days."

Eli laughed and threw an arm around her shoulders. "Come on, I'll help you with dinner, and give you your first lesson."

Saturday dawned hot and muggy. At breakfast Gus and Eli were quick to decline Delilah's invitation to play poker with the girls that evening, claiming a multitude of "vitally important missions" and "countleth engagementth" elsewhere. They would, however, make time to eat pot roast with all the fixings, and a slice of homemade apple pie, in the kitchen, away from the "gaggle of geese" congregated in the dining room.

Delilah filled plates for Gus and Eli that evening, and placed them on the kitchen table, where the two men wasted no time devouring their meal. She spooned the remaining food into bowls and onto platters, and as soon as the meal was laid out on the dining room table, the ladies arrived; Patty and her granddaughter, Sophie, followed by Odie, and then Karon.

Unaware that the back door was the most commonly used entrance to the house, all the ladies had parked in front of the house, and entered through the front door.

"I guess I didn't pay attention when I came out here with Dooby," Karon said as she entered the house. "I went two miles instead of one at that last turn, or I would've been here sooner. So, where's this fella of yours?" she added, looking around.

Delilah shot Karon a reproachful look. "Gus and Eli are eating in the kitchen," she said.

"Well, do I get to meet 'im?" Karon said.

"I suppose so," Delilah said, leading Karon into the dining room.

As the ladies dined, Delilah regaled them with the Arkansas escapades, with particular emphasis on Mordecai Pulapup. Though considerably amused by the old man's eccentricities, Karon was far more interested in additional information about Delilah's involvement with Eli.

"No," Delilah proclaimed for the third time. "There is nothing going on between us. He's marginally arrogant, and an insufferable flirt."

Patty laughed and nodded knowingly. "Yes," she said with fond recollection. "If I remember correctly, he IS quite the handsome charmer."

"So you've met him?" Delilah asked.

"Oh, yes," Patty replied. "Once, just before he left for college, and again about ten years later when he was home from . . . Australia, I believe. Does he still have dreamy eyes?"

At that moment there was a knock on the facing of the door from the entry hall to the dining room. Eli peeped around the opening.

"Good evening, Ladies," he said, entering the room with Gus closely behind him. "Gus and I have agreed to do the dishes for you. Give you more time for poker."

Eli beamed as he caught sight of Patty. "Mrs. Stockton!" he said enthusiastically, stepping toward her. "I didn't know you were part of the group. It's wonderful to see you."

Patty stood and embraced Eli. "I'm quite pleased to see you again, Eli. Fit as ever, I see."

Delilah introduced Eli and Gus to the remaining party. Patty and Karon acknowledged having met Gus before, and Karon commented on Gus's well healed foot.

Eli's charm was not lost on any of the company. It seemed to ooze from every pore of his body as he engaged them all in witted conversation, and propitious flattery. Karon, in particular was taken by his debonair demeanor.

After Eli and Gus cleaned the kitchen, Eli entered the dining room again and told everyone how pleased he was to make their acquaintance. He then excused himself, and turned toward the kitchen.

"Eli," Karon said, "why don't you stay and play poker with us? You can sit here next to me."

A flirtatiously devilish grin inched across Eli's face. "Uh . . . I have to go to the barn to check on . . . something," Eli replied. And with a nod to the ladies, he turned and left the room.

"Mm hmm," Karon sang, as she leaned back in her chair to admire the view of Eli from behind. "Oh Lawd. Look. At. That. Girl, he is fine; for a skinny ass white boy. And those eyes. I never seen eyes that color."

"Karon," Odie said with a whispered chuckle, "he can probably hear you."

"What's your point?" Karon said.

From the kitchen, Eli turned his head and winked at Karon, which immediately produced a rapid two-handed fanning while she continued watching Eli. She continued leaning backward, pushing the stress limits of the chair legs until he was out of her line of vision.

"Are you sure there's nothin' goin' on between the two of you?" Karon asked Delilah, as she shuffled the deck of cards. "Or maybe the appropriate question is WHY is there nothin' goin' on between the two of you?"

Delilah grinned and shook her head.

"Well what's the problem, Girl?" Karon insisted as she dealt the cards. "You've got the means, the opportunity, and all it takes is one look at him for a motive. One-eyed Jacks and suicide Kings, ladies."

"You make it sound like a crime," Sophie said, throwing her nickel in the pot.

Karon's brow shot skyward. "Listen, the crime would be lettin' that yummy dish of vanilla go to waste. I'm just sayin'."

"You miss Dooby, don't you?" Delilah said.

"No!" Karon objected. "Well, maybe a little. And from the sounds of it, it may be awhile before he's back."

"I feel relatively certain Dooby wouldn't expect you to wait around for him," Delilah said.

"Oh, no, he doesn't," Karon offered. "I mean, we've talked about it. It's okay with me if he wants to see someone in Georgia, and he says it's okay if I see someone here."

"Sport sex," Patty said nonchalantly. "Of course if you had BOB, you wouldn't have to worry about that."

Everyone was quiet for a moment.

"Oh, dear," Patty said, blushing. "Have I offended anyone?"

Everyone shook their heads.

"I'm almost afraid to ask," Odie said. "But, who's Bob?"

"Battery Operated Boyfriend," Patty said, brazenly.

They all laughed heartily.

"That's enough about . . . Bob, and Dooby," Karon insisted with wide eyed shock. "I want to hear more about your hunky white boy."

By evening's end, Karon's attention had shifted from Eli to her dwindling sack of coins; that is until Eli entered the house again around 9:30. He made his way through the kitchen and down the hall to the living room, passing the dining room without a glance.

"Eli?" Delilah called out.

Moments later, Eli stepped into the dining room. "Storm coming," he said. "In Oklahoma City, heading this way."

Thirty minutes later, Delilah's guests had departed, and the house and barn had been secured. The temperature had dropped significantly, and the wind had increased as well. The flashes of light and the rumbles that accompanied them were more frequent in the western sky.

"What about Pandora?" Delilah asked as she and Eli made their way quickly from the barn to the house.

"She'll be fine," Eli assured her. "She usually gets in her shed when it storms."

Delilah paused as they reached Pandora's pen. She couldn't see the goat anywhere.

"See," Eli said. "She's already in there."

Once in the house, Delilah joined Eli in the living room where the two monitored the storm's progress on the television. After a deep yawn, Eli assured Delilah there was no need for her to stay up, so she went to her room and got ready for bed.

It seemed the storm hit with full force the moment she clambered into bed. Thunder boomed with each strike of lightning, while the howling wind blew tree limbs against the house. Delilah exited her bed and opened the doors of her armoire so she could see the television. She climbed back in bed, and just as she reached for the remote control, the lights went out.

She grabbed the Maglite behind her night table, and shrugged on her robe. She scurried downstairs to the breaker box in the kitchen, where she was met by Eli who was lighting a few candles.

"Glad your flashlight's working," he said, holding his own Maglite. "Batteries are dead in this one. Hand me yours, will you? I'll check the breaker box."

Eli flipped a few switches in the breaker box, but there was still no power. "Must be the transformer fuse. Check with Gus; see if his electricity's off, too. Then you better report it to the electric company."

Delilah did as she was instructed. She used her cell phone to call Gus. There was no answer at the trailer, so she and Eli assumed the power was out there also. She phoned the electric company and was informed that the storm had caused a line outage, and crews had been dispatched. She relayed the information to Eli.

"Might as well go back to bed, Delilah. There's nothing we can do." Eli said. "It'll pass soon enough."

Delilah nodded, and turned for the hall. Eli blew out the candles, and quickly joined Delilah who was having some difficulty navigating in the darkness. He took hold of her hand, and led her up the stairs. When they reached her bedroom Eli handed her the flashlight. "You take this," he said.

Delilah reached for the flashlight but lost her grip, and it fell with a thud to the floor. They both bent to retrieve it, and as they stood upright again, Eli took a firm hold of Delilah's arms. They were eye to eye; nose to nose, and Eli wasn't budging. Delilah felt the pace of her pounding heart quicken as Eli's expression went from longing to exasperation.

His lips touched her lips; softly at first, as though he was testing the waters. Sensing no resistance from her, he gently took her in his arms and kissed her; a long, slow, passionate kiss, that took her breath away.

"I'm sorry," Eli said as he stepped back. "I shouldn't have done that. Goodnight, Delilah."

Delilah stood in wonderment at her bedroom door long after Eli had gone to his own room and closed the door. She wondered what had just happened. She wondered why it seemed she was always wondering what had just happened with this man. She wondered if it would happen again, or if it was the result of impulse, and never to be repeated. She wondered how long she had been standing there in the dark wondering.

The following morning, after showering, applying a little more make-up than usual, and putting on her very best T-shirt and blue jeans, she traipsed downstairs to the kitchen. As expected, she found Gus sitting at the kitchen table having a cup of coffee and thumbing through The Corridor Magazine.

"Good morning, Gus," she chirped. "Was there any damage from the storm last night?"

"Nope," Gus answered.

"Good," Delilah said, pulling a coffee cup from the cabinet. "Where's Eli? Is he down at the barn?"

"Nope," Gus said. "He'th gone."

"Oh," Delilah said, slightly confused. "He went to town?"

"No," Gus said matter-of-factly. "He took off early thith morning; bagth and all. Didn't thay where he wath going, or when he'd be back."

"Well, I never," Delilah said with an exasperated huff, as she walked down the hall from the kitchen.

No truer words had ever been spoken. Delilah had NEVER been rejected by a man; NEVER had to work to get a man. Contrarily, she had spent the better part of her life turning them away. She had NEVER needed to turn on her charm, because it was just naturally and effortlessly present. She had NEVER had to engage manipulation or stratagem to induce the opposite sex, though it was unlikely she would if circumstances required it.

She gasped as she started up the stairs. "Was it that bad?" she asked herself aloud. "I must be losing my touch. Maybe he just didn't feel what I felt when we kissed." She contemplated this thought as she topped the stairs, and then made her way into her bedroom. "No, he definitely felt something." She stood a moment in the middle of the room. "Why did I come up here?"

Delilah went back down stairs, but not before checking Eli's bedroom, only to discover that most of his belongings were indeed gone. The room looked very much the same as it did when he had arrived just two weeks earlier.

She spent the rest of that day, and the following two days completely perplexed. She questioned if she had been the one to drive him away, or if it had had nothing to do with her at all. She briefly considered the possibility that he was in some sort of trouble, though there had been nothing in his actions or demeanor to suggest such a thing. Additionally, she was struggling with the realization that perhaps she had grown fonder of him than she cared to.

After three more days of absent communication, she was becoming somewhat put out, teetering on angry. By the time Sunday, a week, rolled around, she was concerned about his welfare. She knew his work took him all over the world. And, consequently, she began having visions of him falling off a cliff somewhere remote and exotic, in pursuit of a silly rock. These portentous thoughts prompted her to spend the better part of Sunday evening and night at the computer Googling foreign lands.

"Gus," she started, Monday morning at breakfast. "Is this typical for Eli? I mean, does he usually fly in and out like this without an explanation to anyone? I mean . . . what if he's been hurt or something? How would anyone know?"

"Well," Gus said. "I think Nettie alwayth knew hith planth, But she never told me. Don't worry about Eli, Delilah. He'll be fine."

Delilah went about her daily chores as she had done for the past week, except that she was now making a concerted effort to dismiss the nagging thoughts of Eli's demise; thoughts she had fabricated in her own mind.

That evening Delilah received three phone calls. Each ring sent Delilah racing for the phone in anticipation of the caller being Eli.

The first call was from her father, Big Daddy, who was exercising his parental right to check up on her. He inquired as to her health, well being, and monetary state. Being assured all was well, he concluded the call.

The second call was from Dooby. He too was checking in with Delilah. He brought her up to date on the snails-pace progress of the Raven Wood renovation, and gave her a quick update on his daughters.

Cassidy, the oldest, was planning a two month European excursion with her mother before she returned to medical school in the fall. Delaney, the youngest, wanted no part of it. She had expressed an interest in going to Oklahoma to stay with Aunt Delilah.

"I would love that!" Delilah exclaimed. "When does she get out of school?"

"Just after your birthday," Dooby said. "We'll have to see how things go. I may bring her out the middle of June. Her mother hasn't exactly warmed to the idea."

"You keep working on Mariah, and I'll keep my fingers crossed," Delilah said.

Their call concluded without a word one about Eli. Dooby didn't ask, and Delilah didn't offer. She knew Dooby felt more at ease knowing Eli was there to keep an eye on the situation. She was also painfully aware that if Dooby knew Eli had gone, he'd be more likely to pull up stakes and head back to Oklahoma.

Within a few minutes of disconnecting from Dooby, Karon rang. "Wanna have lunch tomorrow?" she asked.

"Sure," Delilah answered. "I've wanted to try the Sugar Plum Tea Room. How does that sound?"

"Perfect," Karon said. "But my taste buds are leaning more toward Mexican food. Have you ever eaten at Mi Casa in Stroud?"

At lunch the following day, Delilah nonchalantly confided in Karon the sudden and unexplainable disappearance of Eli, omitting the part about being kissed by him the night before.

Karon gasped. "I'll bet he's a spy!" she exclaimed, scooping more hot sauce onto her taco.

"He's not a spy," Delilah said shaking her head. "He's a geologist."

"Mm, hmm. A geologist," Karon said with a marked degree of skeptical sarcasm. "Right. Which of course would be the perfect cover for a spy."

"You have done lost your mind, sister," Delilah said after a brief pause in which she was scrutinizing Karon's mental capacity, and resisting the urge to laugh.

Karon leaned in closer to Delilah. "Think about it," she whispered excitedly. "He shows up, out of the blue; then leaves without a word, all mysterious like. You said yourself he had a tendency to be evasive. You have no idea how to reach him, or who exactly he works for. The only thing you do know is that he travels a lot. The dude's a spy. I'm just sayin'."

"Yeah, well, my fifth husband traveled a lot, too. He wasn't a spy. Turns out he was just a bigamist," Delilah said.

Karon winced. "Yeah, that was unfortunate," she said. "But I don't see Eli as the bigamist type. He's more like the spy type."

"Thank you, Karon," Delilah said. "That's just what I need; something else to obsess about."

Karon drove Delilah back to the ranch beating the Eli-is-a-spy horse half to death.

"You've got company," Karon said as they pulled around to the garage.

"That's my attorney," Delilah said with some surprise.

Herbert stood beside his Cadillac Escalade engaged in conversation with Gus. He pushed his glasses up the rim of his nose, and adjusted his red bowtie, as Delilah and Karon stepped from Karon's Ford Mustang.

"Delilah!" Herbert sang out. "I have some money for you."

Herbert reached in his car and clumsily pulled a check from his tan leather briefcase while he explained. "This is in response to my letter to the insurance company in regards to the reimbursement for your well house and propane tank."

He handed Delilah the check. "Evidently, they WERE covered by the policy," he added with an odd giggle and a snort. "I know you're struggling with finances, so this should be of some help."

"WAS struggling," Delilah said as she examined the check. "I received a nice little sum for stud fees a couple weeks ago from two ranchers in Arkansas. Thank you, Herbert, for bringing this out to me."

"Who were the ranchers?" Herbert inquired, fidgeting with his bowtie.

"Some ranchers Eli knew. They had done business with Aunt Nettie in the past." Delilah replied, folding the check, and dropping it in her purse.

"Eli?" Herbert asked, slightly startled. "So, Eli's back?"

"He was," Delilah said. "Showed up several weeks back, and then disappeared about a week ago."

"Oh. I wish I'd known," Herbert said with a puzzled expression. "I have some business to discuss with him."

Apologizing for her slacked manners, Delilah introduced Herbert and Karon, and then invited the attorney to join them inside for iced tea. Herbert declined the invitation, and departed with a wave.

"Squirrely little guy, isn't he?" Karon said as they entered the back door to the house.

Delilah smiled. "Yes. But really very sweet," she said. She was lost for a moment in the memory of the night Herbert had proposed to her.

She laughed, recalling his flailing arms and legs as the sofa tipped over. When Karon inquired as to what was so funny, Delilah simply stated that he was an amusing man.

After a couple glasses of tea, Karon left the ranch and Delilah set about taking inventory of the pantry and refrigerator. Her milk and bread supply was low, and there were a few other items that needed replenished.

Delilah had been a city girl most of her adult life, which meant that she could just jump in the car and pop down to the local grocery store with little or no inconvenience. But now that she lived in the country, her shopping experiences were considerably more challenging. She had to make lists, and think ahead. She learned her lesson after a couple times of driving all the way to town, shopping, and then driving all the way back home only to discover she was out of ketchup, or worse, toilet paper.

The following morning, Delilah dressed in a multi-colored sun dress, slipped on a pair of sandals, gathered her grocery list and purse, and set off for town. She pulled away from the garage in her '96 Ford pickup, and started down the hill. When Delilah applied the brakes to slow her descent, the brake pedal went all the way to floor with no resistance.

"OH, SHIT!" Delilah shouted as her mind rapidly raced through her options.

"OH, SHIT!" she shouted again as the vehicle picked up speed, and she frantically pumped the brakes.

She was nearing the bottom of the hill and the bridge at a dangerously fast pace. She had to make a choice, and make it quickly; the creek, or a hundred year old sycamore tree. She chose the creek, and pulled the emergency brake.

The pickup came to a bumpy stop about twenty feet off the drive, and two feet short of the creek bank. She let go the breath she had been holding since making her choice, and sat a moment gathering her composure.

After locating Gus, and changing into work clothes, the two used his pickup to tow hers back to the garage, where a large puddle of brake fluid was discovered on the concrete pad.

Delilah watched as Gus checked under the hood. This had happened to her once before when she was in college, and although that incident had been mechanical failure, a sinking suspicion now sat uncomfortably in the pit of her stomach.

"Gus?" Delilah broached hesitantly. "Can you tell if someone's tampered with the brakes?"

Gus's head jerked out from under the hood. "You think . . ." he said with a horrified expression.

Delilah, clearly frustrated, rubbed her forehead with both hands. "I don't know. I mean . . . there could be a perfectly logical explanation, I guess? I'm probably just being paranoid, right?"

Gus wiped his hands on his blue jeans, and then patted Delilah on the arm. "Not paranoid. Cautiouth. I can't tell if there'th been any tampering," he said with genuine concern.

Still slightly shaken, Delilah opted to postpone her trip to town until the following day.

After waking to a warm, cloudless day, Delilah decided to drive Nettie's '67 Camaro 427 convertible. It had been locked in the garage, safe, secure, and tamper-proof. And sure enough, her trip to town was free of mishaps; the exception being her initial adjustment to driving a standard four on the floor. Once she got the hang of it, she rather enjoyed the vehicle's power. She came to understood Aunt Nettie's fondness for it, and the general appreciation shared by most men.

"WOO HOO!" she shouted gleefully as she laid rubber at the intersection of Highway 99 and Highway 33. "YES!"

She basked in the attention she got from passers-by in town, knowing full well it was the car turning heads. If she heard "nice car" once, she heard it a half dozen times.

Once home, she parked her new found toy in the garage, unloaded the groceries, and began supper; all the while contemplating a name for the vehicle.

"I'm trying to think of a name for her, Gus," Delilah said, after telling him about the thrill of driving the car that day. "She should have a spicy, peppy name."

Gus laughed as he spooned mashed potatoes and gravy into his mouth. "She ith peppy, for sure," he said. "A lotta car in a little package."

Delilah's eyes brightened with comprehension. "That's it! Carlotta!" she declared with a hint of a Spanish accent, and a snap of her fingers.

After breakfast the next day, Delilah and Gus mended a small stretch of fence, brush-hogged an overgrown spot of pasture, and worked the ponies. Even Pandora had participated in these efforts, riding along side Delilah on the tractor, and herding the horses.

"She thinks she's a Border Collie," Delilah told Gus as they returned to the barn to straighten up and lock up that evening. "I have a goat with a canine complex."

As the two entered the barn, a glint of something about three inches above the ground, and eight feet away, caught Delilah's eye. It became clearer as she stepped closer, and she followed the line of it. It ran from one side of the barn to the other.

"Gus, did you string this wire across the ground?" Delilah said, reaching down toward the wire. "What in the world?"

"Delilah! No!" Gus shouted lunging toward her.

But it was too late. Delilah had already given the wire a forceful tug.

Chapter 9

Dead Man's Hand

With tremendous force, Gus took hold of Delilah, and pushed her forward, covering her as they landed on the ground, while simultaneously a half dozen large bales of hay fell from the loft above, and landed in the very spot where Delilah had just been standing.

Forty-five minutes later, the Lincoln County Sheriff was standing in the barn looking over the rigging of the wire trap, while his deputy was dusting for finger prints.

"Not getting anything, Charlie," the deputy said. "Must've wiped it down. There aren't any prints at all."

The sheriff nodded confirmation of what he appeared to already know. He turned to Delilah. "Tell me, Delilah," he said as he studied the notes on his pad. "Did anything suspicious happen while Eli was here?"

Delilah knew instantly where the sheriff was going with this line of questioning. "No!" she answered defiantly. "Well, except for that note on Pandora's pin. You don't honestly think Eli has anything to do with this, do you?"

"No!" the sheriff responded, after a moment's hesitation. "Not exactly. I'm just wondering if the perpetrator knew he was here, and waited until he was gone to make his move, which would mean . . ." The sheriff stopped and looked sternly into Delilah's eyes. "They're watching you."

This did not surprise Delilah. She had often felt like she was being watched. And from the expression on the sheriff's face, he wasn't surprised either.

The officers concluded their investigation, and accompanied Delilah and Gus back to the house, where she offered them a choice of soda, or tea. Taking the sodas, the two men sat down at the kitchen table with Delilah and Gus, and began questioning them again, taking notes as the answers were given. In the midst of the interview, Gus passively mentioned the failing brakes on the pickup a few days earlier.

"What?" the sheriff said in astonished disbelief. He quickly exchanged a furtive glance with the deputy, and then asked the deputy to check the pickup.

The deputy exited the house with Gus in tow, who was explaining that he had already made the repairs and hadn't seen any signs of tampering.

"Delilah," the sheriff said in a low voice, "how well do you know Gus?"

"You can't be serious!" Delilah said indignantly. "You've just crossed the line sheriff. I'd believe anyone else in the world capable of this before I'd believe Gus was the culprit."

"Now don't get mad," the sheriff said. "I have to consider everyone. Sometimes I even have to consider the least obvious."

Delilah smiled at the public servant and said with her silkiest, Georgia peach, drawl, "Gus would certainly qualify as the least obvious. And as far as I'm concerned you're grasping at straws."

The sheriff smiled. "That's all I wanted to hear," he said.

Delilah chose to keep the sheriff's comment to herself and not burden the toothless ranch hand with it. Instead, she let the accusation simmer in her mind over the next few days. She understood it was his job to suspect everyone. But how could he possibly suspect Gus? It wasn't as though he was some transient who'd shown up recently. He'd been on the ranch for years. Aunt Nettie had obviously trusted him, and so did Delilah. And, although the sheriff was quick to deny suspicion of Eli, the split second hesitation, and the miniscule uncertainty of his tone, forced Delilah to doubt the sincerity of his denial.

Monday morning brought a call from Herbert, the attorney.

"Delilah," Herbert said. "I wonder, have you heard from Eli yet?"

Try as she might to forget Eli, it seemed there was always some reminder of him. This was no exception. "No," Delilah replied.

"Well, the other day when I brought you the check, I failed to ask you to notify me when he returns. Or, better yet, if you would just have him contact me when you see or hear from him next."

"Of course," Delilah agreed.

"Is there something wrong, Dear?" Herbert inquired. "You sound . . . out of sorts."

Delilah made some feeble excuse for her curt tone. But then decided perhaps it was in her best interest to share these experiences with her attorney. So, she told him about the pickup brakes, and the barn incident.

There was a long stretch of silence in which Delilah thought the connection had been broken. She called out Herbert's name.

"Oh, yes Dear. I'm sorry," he said a bit addled. "Oh, my! That sounds exactly like something Murray Rockford would do. You remember me telling you about Murray? He's not very bright. Oh, my!" Herbert rattled on as though he was talking to himself. "And his situation IS becoming more desperate. But of course that's privileged information."

Completely distracted, Herbert concluded his call. Delilah went about her chores that day with the ever present thought of Murray Rockford nagging away at her nearly as often as thoughts of Eli.

Apart from several severe thunderstorms, the rest of the week was smooth sailing. The lightning and thunder reminded Delilah of the night before Eli departed, and she found that she missed him more on those occasions. But her longing for him was tempered by self-reprobation. She continued to tell herself that she had only really known him a couple weeks, which was not enough time to really know someone at all.

Anti-Eli, sitting on her left shoulder, reminded her of how annoying he could be, and evasive, and obviously irresponsible. While Pro-Eli, who sat on her right shoulder, pointed out that he was funny, intelligent, and on occasion thoughtful, not to mention cute. Determined to forget about him altogether, she simply practiced dismissing any thought of him the second it popped into her head.

"Aren't you going to the Senior Citizen's dance in Cushing tonight?" Delilah asked Gus, Friday evening at supper.

"I think I better thtay here," Gus said pleasantly.

"Gus," Delilah said practically scolding him. "You haven't been to Cushing on Friday night in weeks. Go. I've got the sheriff on speed dial, and an arsenal in the gun cabinet. Go."

Gus laughed. "I don't have a lot of confidenth in your ability to uthe the arthenal," he said.

"You mean because I shot you in the foot?" Delilah said, laughing. "I'll never live that down, will I?"

"No," Gus said, laughing along with her. "Why don't you come with me?"

After a moment's hesitation, she answered. "Alright, I will. I haven't been dancing in years. Might be fun. I'll be ready in forty-five minutes."

She hustled up the stairs, showered, fixed her hair and makeup, and slipped into a knee length, red silk floral dress with a full skirt. She pulled on her Jimmy Choos, and bound down the stairs.

Oh what fun it was; except for the glares Delilah got from the little old ladies who were sweet on Gus. One woman in particular, approached Delilah and asked her who she was and how long she had been dating Gus. Delilah's explanation of her connection to him seemed to satisfy the woman only marginally. And then there were the other women who appeared to resent Delilah when their partners asked Delilah to dance.

All in all, Delilah did have a good time. She enjoyed the band, The Thunderbirds, and by the end of the evening, she was at least on speaking terms with the ladies.

"Boy, they sure are territorial," Delilah said with a laugh as they drove back to the ranch. "I have to say, though, I was quite impressed with their agility. And the song Shake, Rattle and Roll has a whole new meaning, now. Did you see that one woman do the splits?"

"Which one?" Gus asked.

"The one with purple hair," Delilah said.

"Mary Lou," Gus said with a chuckle. "Yeah, she'th about 80 yearth old, and quite popular."

Delilah's eyes went wide. "Ya don't say."

They arrived at the ranch, keyed in the combination to the security gate, and made their way up the winding drive. Delilah bounded from the pickup and waved to Gus, who remained parked in the drive until she got in the house. Once she flipped the light on in the kitchen, Gus drove on to his trailer a few hundred yards beyond the barn.

Delilah stood at the kitchen sink, looking through the window, and watched Gus drive off. For some reason, call it intuition, the atmosphere in the house felt different. A chill instinctively ran up her spine. She dropped her purse on the counter top as she reached in a cabinet drawer and pulled out a butcher knife.

She slowly inched her way down the hall holding the knife up and positioned to stab if need be. She slowly peeked in the dining room, the bathroom, and then the living room; turning on lights as she went. Gratified that the first floor was absent of intruders, she inched her way up the stairs, and found the second floor lifeless, as well.

She breathed a deep, cleansing sigh of relief. "This is crazy," she said irritably, as she stomped back down the stairs. "I'm a paranoid, nervous wreck. He won't have to kill me to get me off the ranch. Much more of this and I'll wind up at the funny farm."

She returned the knife to the drawer in the kitchen, swung her purse over her shoulder, and made her way back down the hall, turning the lights off as she went. When she reached the living room, something caught her eye that had gone unnoticed with her first investigation. A window pane had been broken.

The sheriff was there bright and early the next morning. Delilah had gone through the house and found nothing missing. There was no indication that the perpetrator had entered the house. At this point, the sheriff suggested she have an alarm system or security cameras installed. Delilah said she would consider it but the only advantage she could see to either option would be that the sheriff would be more expeditiously notified when Mr. Creepy killed her.

"Sheriff," Delilah said.

"Why don't you call me Charlie?" he replied. "I think we know each other well enough to be on a first name basis."

"Okay," Delilah agreed. "If that's the case, then we know each other well enough for me to be perfectly candid."

"Like that's ever been a problem," he said with a hint of a smile.

After a tilt of her head, a pursing of the lips, and a brief disapproving look, Delilah continued. "Is Murray Rockford a suspect?"

Charlie studied Delilah a moment. "Yes," he said. "A very strong suspect."

"Well, why don't you just arrest him?" Delilah said, slightly agitated.

"Delilah, you're a pretty smart ole gal," Charlie said. "You know I can't arrest someone on a hunch. Suspicion is one thing; evidence is another. As witless as Murray is, he seems to be smart enough to leave a crime scene clean. There's also another alternative, albeit remote. There's the issue of your cousin in Macon."

This took Delilah by surprise.

"I DO talk to Dooby," Charlie said as he walked to the back door.

"Charlie," Delilah called out. "Thank you. I'm sorry to be such a pest."

"You're not a pest," Charlie said with a laugh. "Mrs. Blauckmore in Chandler is a pest. She sees little green men coming out of her electrical outlets about twice a week. On my way there now."

Delilah chuckled, and waved him out the door thankful she wasn't seeing little green men . . . yet.

Three days later, Delilah was getting an estimate for a security system. Much to her chagrin, she felt the cost was too exorbitant, unless of course, they could install a system with portable AK-47's at each corner of the house that would automatically fire at anything that came within a 30 yard radius of the structure. In jest, the security man explained that that option was only availably to drug lords and high ranking political officials.

Late the following night, however, she reconsidered her choice when she was awakened by the rattle of the knob on the back door.

She jumped from her bed, grabbed her Maglite, and ran to the bedroom window facing the drive way. She opened the shutters just in time to see a tall, dark figure running down the drive toward the road, with Pandora's horns dangerously close to the man's behind.

"This is absurd!" she said, ranting to the sheriff the next day.

"The odd thing is," Charlie said with a troubled sigh. "I had a man out here watching the place two nights before. Couldn't spare him last night."

"Well, Sheriff, looks like I'm not the only one being watched," Delilah said. "Or, you've just become a suspect, too."

Delilah needed a diversion. Between Mr. Creepy and Eli, she was swiftly coming to the end of her rope. Shopping or poker. Perhaps the level of stress she was currently enduring would require both. As soon as Charlie left, she was on the phone to Karon, insisting on the poker option.

"Well, I know Sophie's in California negotiating a movie option for one of her screen plays," Karon said. "But, I don't think there'll be a problem getting Patty and Odie to play. I'll call them."

"Good," Delilah said. "Saturday night, my house. And by the way, what are you doing tomorrow afternoon?"

After hearing Delilah's plight, Karon agreed to take off work Friday afternoon for a little shopping trip. By 2:00 the next day, Karon was pulling up the drive at the ranch.

Karon stepped out of her black Mustang wearing skin tight blue jeans, a black, off the shoulder poet's shirt, and four inch, spike, leopard print high heels. She topped off the ensemble with a leopard print head wrap, and three inch, gold hoop earrings. She was patting the top of her head as she walked toward Delilah, who was coming out the back door.

"New weave?" Delilah asked with a smile.

"How'd you know?" Karon asked.

"I'd like to check out Old Songs Sung Here, in Cushing," Delilah said as they loaded into the Mustang.

"Antiques?" Karon questioned incredulously. "Really? I guess you DO like antiques. You got a lot of them. Me? I've never been that fond of old things. Just the thought of

208

other people, lots of other people usin' things, and gettin' their body oils and Lord knows what else all over . . . well, it just don't appeal to me at all. I'm just sayin'."

Delilah and Karon arrived in downtown Cushing and parked in front of Old Songs Sung Here. A small sign that read 'Warning, Crazy Cat', hung on the old screen door. Delilah chuckled at the sign and opened the door.

"I ain't goin' in there," Karon said, vigorously shaking her head. "I don't like cats. Cats give me the heebie-jeebies. Especially crazy cats. Cats and grasshoppers. Always jumpin' around."

"Will you stop?" Delilah said, taking Karon's arm and pulling her inside.

Upon entering the store they were greeted by a white haired woman with wire-rimmed glasses, and a broad smile.

"Hello, Ladies," she said. "I'm Connie. If you need help finding anything, just let me know." And then she crowed like a rooster.

Karon's eyes went wide. "Oh, I get it," she whispered. "She's the cat that's crazy."

Delilah pulled Karon down an isle between two shelves that stood seven feet high, with dolls on one side, and linens on the other.

"Girlfriend?" Connie called from the cash register.

Delilah and Karon exchanged glances. "Who's she talking to," Karon asked. "We're the only ones in the store."

Delilah shrugged and shook her head.

"Girlfriend, where are you?" Connie called again.

"Maybe her girlfriend is a ghost," Delilah said with a grin.

"Are you kidding me?" Karon said with a whispered shriek. "First a cat, and now a ghost? I am gettin' out of here!"

At that moment, four shelves up, between the Chatty Cathy doll and the Mrs. Beasley doll, there swiftly emerged the paw of an enormous tabby, which sucker punched Karon's ear.

Karon shrieked, and screamed, "Sweet Jesus," while Connie stepped around the corner and said, "Girlfriend, how many times have I told you not to scare people?"

Connie pulled the cat from the shelf.

Delilah laughed and nodded. "The cat's name is Girlfriend," she told Karon who was patting her chest with one hand, and rubbing her ear with the other.

"That cat just sucker punched me!" Karon said.

"No she didn't," Connie said. "She was just trying to love on you. See?" Connie turned the feline towards Karon, and the cat reached for Karon's cheek once again.

Karon put a hand up to stop the gesture. "That's nice. That's real nice."

After patronizing several other stores downtown, the pair agreed on Mr. Lu's for supper, followed by a movie at the Dunkin Theater. And by 10:00, Karon was pulling up the drive at the ranch.

"You make a pretty good date," Karon said as she put the idling car into park. "Just don't expect a kiss."

Delilah laughed.

"Listen," Karon said seriously. "I'm kinda worried about you out here all alone, what with everything that's goin' on. You're welcome to stay at Camp Karon, if you like."

"Camp Karon?" Delilah repeated with a laugh.

"Yeah," Karon said. "That's what the nieces and nephews call my place, 'cause there's sleepin' bags and sheet tents all over the house when they come stay. The older ones think it's Karon-Mart. 'I'm out of toilet paper. Got any laundry soap? Where's the light bulbs?'" Karon said in a mocking voice.

After a moment of laughter, Delilah assured Karon she would be fine, and stepped out of the car. She went in the house, turned on the kitchen light, and then waved Karon on.

Before going to bed, Delilah placed a tower of pots and pans at the front and back doors; her idea of an inexpensive security system. And she strung a wire across the bottom of the French doors to the screened porch; Mr. Creepy's idea of tripping someone up.

Bright and early the next morning, she was back downstairs removing the metal from the back door before Gus showed up for breakfast. The bacon had been sizzling only five minutes when Gus came lopping through the door waving a note.

"Better take a look at thith, Delilah," he said, handing her the grimy piece of paper. "It wath hanging on the back door."

'Just a matter of time' was all it said in the same hen-scratched writing as all of the previous notes. Delilah picked up the phone, and called Charlie.

"No," Delilah said to Charlie after telling him what had been found. "Don't come out. I'll just save this until I see you again. I don't mind saying, Sheriff, I'm quickly becoming irritated with all of this. It won't take much more for me to go from frightened to angry. And you may as well know . . . an angry Delilah is NOT a pretty sight."

The rest of the day was spent mowing the lawn, and weed eating. And the poor, defenseless weeds in the flower beds, fell victim to Delilah's wrath. When Delilah and Gus finished the yard work around the house, they went to Gus's trailer and did the same there.

A hot and sweaty Delilah jumped in the shower late that afternoon, and emerged refreshed and ready to prepare dinner for her three poker guests.

The ladies arrived a couple hours later and feasted on Chicken Fettuccini Alfredo, garlic bread, and tossed salad.

"I think you need to tell Patty and Odie what's been going on around here," Karon whispered to Delilah, as the four women removed the dishes from the table, and took them to the kitchen.

"Maybe later," Delilah said in a low voice. "I don't want to kill the mood."

Karon nodded. Everyone gathered around the table again, and Patty began shuffling the deck of cards.

"Shame Eli had to leave so abruptly," Patty said as she dealt the cards. "Ok Ladies, everyone's anteed up. We're playing POPs. Plain Old Poker, five card draw, open on guts."

Delilah bet a nickel on her hand. "I'm sure he had something important to do," she said, as everyone added their bet.

Karon rolled her eyes. "Mm hmm," she said, discarding. "Three cards, please."

"Karon thinks he's a spy," Delilah said with a smile. "Two cards for me."

"A spy?" Odie shrieked. "I'll take one card."

"And the dealer takes three," Patty said, pulling three cards off the top of the deck.

"What makes you think he's a spy?" Odie asked incredulously, as she threw a coin in the pot. "Nickle."

"He's just so mysterious," Karon said spookily, as all the players added their nickels to the pot. "Comin' and goin' all stealth like. Always changin' the subject when you ask him questions. The dude's a spy. I'm just sayin'."

"Oh for cryin' out loud, Karon!" Odie said with raucous laughter. She laid her hand down. "Two pair, aces and eights."

"Also known as dead man's hand," Patty offered. "I'm out."

"Also known as Delilah's matrimonial history," Delilah added, tossing her under turned cards on top of the deck.

Everyone laughed.

"It's the mark of a strong woman who can make light of five dead husbands," Patty said, as she gathered the cards and handed them to Odie, who was raking her winnings toward her.

"It's either laugh or cry," Delilah said. "And trust me I did my fair share of crying."

Karon quickly addressed the spy issue again to continued appalled reactions from Odie. And each time, throughout the evening, when these volleys occurred, Delilah noticed a peculiar expression on Patty's face. Not only was she completely unabashed by these revelations, but she actually appeared to be suppressing a smile; and not the smile of someone who was amused, but the smile of someone who knew a secret.

By evenings end, Karon had let go of the spy theory, and found a new bone to chew on.

"Delilah has a stalker," Karon announced to a totally unprepared audience.

Once the silencing shock wore off, the interrogation began. Who? What? When? Why?

Delilah grudgingly went through the list of mishaps that had taken place just since Eli's departure. "And then this morning Gus found a nasty little note on the back door," she concluded, sending a furtive look at Karon. "I'm not certain who it is, so consequently I can't be certain why. Initially I was unnerved, of course. But now, I'm tending more towards angry."

"Did you know your aunt had a problem with Murray Rockford at one time?" Patty said without hesitation. "Forgive me. I probably shouldn't accuse anyone."

"Don't apologize," Delilah said, reassuringly. "As a matter of fact, he's the primary suspect."

Patty shared all she knew about the feud between Murray and Nettie, all of which Delilah had already been made aware of. As poker night concluded all three ladies offered to stay with Delilah or put her up at their own homes until the matter was resolved. Delilah graciously declined the invitations, and they all said good night.

After her guests departed, Delilah repeated the pots and pans drill she had preformed the night before, and went upstairs. She checked the Maglite tucked behind her night table, and discovered a dimming light. She placed the flashlight on the table to remind her the following morning to change the batteries, and then went to bed. Again she had fitful dreams, and interrupted sleep, and a vague awareness of an aching neck and shoulders.

Delilah woke Sunday morning with a scratchy throat and watery eyes. She shrugged on her robe, grabbed the flashlight on the bedside table and headed downstairs where she phoned Gus and told him not to come to the house unless he wanted to wind up sick, too. As the day progressed, so did her cold, and by night fall, she was simply miserable.

Karon phoned that evening in search of her sunglasses, which Delilah couldn't find, though her search was lackadaisical. After insinuating that Delilah sounded like a three-pack-a-day frog on a four day whiskey binge, Delilah politely sneezed in Karon's ear, and then concluded the call. Shortly thereafter, she went about turning the lights off down stairs. She had stayed inside all day, and Gus had stayed away, so the pots and pans had not been moved from the night before.

After a long hot bath, Delilah took a dose of Nyquil, and for good measure, an extra long swig from the bottle. She climbed into bed, and was out like a light within minutes. She was sleeping soundly and peacefully until she was awakened by the sound of metal clanging on the kitchen floor. She sat straight up in bed. Someone was in the house.

She fumbled for the phone, and dialed Gus's number at the trailer as she bolted from her bed, grabbed her robe, and looked out her window. There were no cars in the drive.

"Get up here," she whispered frantically when Gus answered the phone. "Someone's in the house."

The pots had stopped clanking, and she could hear footsteps, of the two legged variety, in the hall downstairs. It wasn't Pandora. She groped behind the bedside table for her Maglite, and then remembered she'd left it in the kitchen after changing the batteries. She scanned the dark bedroom for an optional weapon. Nothing. The intruder had started up the stairs. Terrified, Delilah quickly tip-toed into the adjoining bathroom and armed herself with the only thing available. The plunger.

She crouched behind the door from the bathroom to the hall. The man topped the stairs, and with a blood curdling battle cry, she charged at him in the darkness with the plunger. She whacked him over the head with it, and then plunged it into his chest, sending him tumbling backward down the stairs.

Chapter 10

Another Dead Man's Hand

"Delilah!" the man called out as he went tumbling backward down the stairs.

Delilah reached behind her and flipped on the hall light. "Oh, damn! Eli!"

She raced down the stairs with the plunger still in hand, and knelt beside him, all the while asking if he was alright.

"What did you do that for?" Eli whined, grasping his left elbow.

"I thought you were the creep that's been terrorizing me," she replied. "Turns out you're the other creep," she added haughtily, once she realized he wasn't severely injured.

"Well that remotely explains the cook ware at the back door," he surmised.

"What are you doing here?" she snapped harshly.

"I live here!" he shouted. "Don't I?"

"That's a good question," she snapped back as she helped him to his feet. "You left without a word. I haven't seen or heard from you in weeks. For all I knew you could've fallen off a cliff in Egypt or Bora Bora."

"Well, Egypt is desert, and Bora Bora is a tropical island," Eli corrected. He looked down at the contents of Delilah's hand, and said sarcastically, "a plunger, Delilah? Really?"

Just as Delilah was ready to remind him of the damage the plunger inflicted, Gus came bounding in the back door, wearing bright red long handles and slip-on house shoes, wielding his sawed-off 870 Remington shot gun, and shouting Delilah's name.

"We're in here," Delilah and Eli replied in unison.

"Is that loaded, Gus?" Eli asked as he limped to the living room.

"Yeah," Gus answered breathlessly, nodding his head. "Double 00 buckshot."

"Now THAT'S a weapon," Eli said to Delilah.

"Yeah?" Delilah said, confrontationally, traipsing after Eli. "You better be glad I used a plunger on you instead of THAT!" she continued to shout as she pointed at Gus with her plunger, and wiped the snot from her nose with the back of her free hand. "Otherwise we wouldn't be having this conversation. I'd be calling Charlie and making arrangements to have you removed by the coroner."

"I doubt it!" Eli fired back as he plopped down on the sofa. "From what I understand, you can't hit the broad side of a barn, unless you're aiming at a target at least fifty yards away from it."

Delilah's furrowed brow was accentuated by her drop-jawed gasp of air. But as she recalled her one and only attempt at target practice, and the number of holes in the side of the barn, put there by her while attempting to shoot a target approximately fifty yards away, a smile crept across her face, and she began nodding. "That's funny, actually."

Eli flashed his flirtatious smile at Delilah, and patted the sofa; his idea of an invitation to join him. Gus excused himself, and went out the back door.

"And by the way," Delilah said as she plopped down on the sofa. "Bora Bora is a volcanic island, so it DOES have cliffs. I looked it up."

"So, how long have you been referring to the sheriff as Charlie?" Eli asked.

"Well, I've talked to him so frequently lately that all manner of propriety has been dismissed," Delilah said with a heavy sigh, and a long sniff.

"What do you mean?" Eli said with a jerk of his head and accusing look.

"It's not what you think," Delilah said, reading the implication in Eli's tone and expression. "Mr. Creepy has taken advantage of your absence. From practically the moment you abandoned me, he's doubled his efforts to terrorize me. Where have you been, by the way? No! Don't tell me. I don't want to know."

In actuality, there was a part of her that did want to know where he'd been, and what he'd been doing; why he'd left so abruptly. If her own natural curiosity wasn't enough, Karon's insane speculation that he was a spy had added fuel to the fire.

"I suspect you wouldn't tell me even if I DID want to know, would you?" she said resentfully.

Eli sighed, and looked genuinely troubled. "No," he said.

"It's alright," she said with a sniffle. "I'll admit I was confused, at first, even a bit angry; more than anything because I was left hanging. And I wondered if it was me."

Eli started to say something, but Delilah held up her hand to stop him.

"I was also worried . . . about you," she said, reaching in the pocket of her robe for a Kleenex. "But, you're okay. Obviously."

"So," Eli said slowly. "What's been going on here?"

After a triple sneeze, and the expulsion of a lung, Delilah filled him in on all that had happened in his absence.

"Charlie seems cautiously certain it's that Rockford guy," Delilah said, wiping her nose with the Kleenex. "He just doesn't have enough hard evidence to arrest him, and he hasn't been able to catch him yet. He thinks I need to get a security camera. But even then, there's no guarantee we'll be able to see who it is." Delilah sneezed again.

Eli had listened in stony silence. His expression offered no surprise, indignation, rage, or emotion of any sort. He held a hand to Delilah's forehead, and then touched her cheek. "You're hot. You need to get back to bed."

Delilah nodded and grinned. "Normally I'd be turned on by a statement like that," she said, pulling herself up from the sofa. She started toward the foyer, coughing as she went.

"Do you have medicine?" Eli asked.

"Nyquil," she answered as she started her climb up the stairs.

"I'm right behind you," Eli said.

Minutes later she was crawling into bed, and Eli was pouring her another dose of liquid sleep. She knocked back the capful, and with a shiver, slinked down under the covers.

"Can I get you anything else?" Eli said sweetly as he tucked the covers under her chin.

She blinked feverishly, fighting the weight of her eyelids. She shook her head.

"Alright," Eli said. "Good night."

As he got to her bedroom door, Delilah called out his name. He stopped and turned toward her.

"I really am glad you're back," she said dreamily.

"Me, too," he said. And then he went to his bedroom.

Delilah slept late the following morning. It was nearly 10:00 when she finally rose, and took a long hot shower. She felt marginally better, but knew she shouldn't over exert, at the risk of relapsing.

When she reached the kitchen, she found a note from Eli. "Gone to town, E." She made a pot of hot tea and a piece of toast. After consuming the tea and toast, she refilled her cup and went to the living room.

She sat down at the massive, old, oak desk, and tugged and pulled the lap drawer until it finally gave way. She extracted her accounts register, and tossed it atop the desk. The phone rang. It was Karon.

"How you feeling, Girl?" Karon asked sympathetically.

"Better," Delilah answered with a sniff.

"You don't sound better," Karon offered. "I'm goin' to the store. Thought I'd call to see if you needed anything."

"Well, thanks for checking on me, but I'm fine," Delilah said. "Besides, guess who's back."

"Dooby?" Karon guessed with excitement.

"Sorry, no," Delilah said.

"Oh, the spy," Karon said with a hint of bitterness. "Did he have an explanation for his sudden disappearance?"

"We haven't talked about it," Delilah said. "It's really none of my business anyway."

"Mm hmm," Karon said. "I'd get to the bottom of this, if I were you. He shouldn't treat you like that. I don't care how cute he is. It ain't right. And you know how guys are. If you let 'em get away with one little thing then they think it's permission to do other stupid shit. I'm just sayin'."

About that time, she saw Eli through the window, pulling up the drive. She promised to check in with Karon later, and hung up.

Delilah listened as Eli came in the back door, and eventually made his way down the hall, stopping as he reached the living room.

"Oh," he said cheerfully, as he entered the room. "You're up. How do you feel?"

"A little better," she said, remaining seated at the desk, while Eli plopped in the chair closest to her.

"Look, Delilah," he began, nervously. He leaned in closer, and placed his elbows on his knees. "I know I owe you an apology for taking off without an explanation. And at some point I may be able to tell you why . . ."

"You don't owe me anything," Delilah said calmly. She took a deep breath. "Your business is none of my business, Eli. I mean, unless you want it to be. And I'm okay with that. I won't pry or interfere. I understand that you have obligations outside the ranch. And I understand that sometimes a man just needs to get away to the 'man cave'. My only request is that you simply tell me you're going the next time you go; BEFORE you go."

Eli appraised Delilah. With a deep breath, and what appeared to be a great struggle, he said, "I . . ." He stopped, and with a smile of resignation he finished. "Deal."

Eli rose from his chair, insisting that Delilah get comfortable on the sofa while he prepared his famous cure-all chicken noodle soup, which he served twenty minutes later, along with iced tea and mixed fruit. He rummaged through the DVD cabinet, extracted a romantic comedy, and popped it into the DVD player.

Eli left Delilah snug in her little sofa cocoon, went upstairs, and a few minutes later came back downstairs with a basket of laundry, which he took to the kitchen, and loaded into the washing machine. After the laundry was started, he returned to the living room, and asked Delilah if there was anything else he could get her.

"No," she said suspiciously. "Thank you."

Eli's cell phone rang. He looked at the display, and after a barely perceptible pause, he answered the call. "This is Eli," he said with a quick glance at Delilah, who turned her attention back to the movie.

"That fast?" Eli said as he turned and started out of the room. "No, it's not a problem for me. Let's do it," he continued as he walked down the hall, out of ear shot from Delilah.

At this point all Delilah could hear was mumbling. Not that she was listening. Okay, maybe she WAS listening.

Once his call was concluded, Eli excused himself, and went to the barn.

That evening, after another round of chicken soup, Eli insisted Delilah retire early. Around 9:00 he tucked her into bed, poured an extra dose of Nyquil down her, and gave her a little pill "guaranteed" to make her well.

Having slept like a rock, Delilah woke early the following morning, feeling much better. The river of sinus mucus had finally stopped flowing, and she felt well rested. After a quick shower, she threw on a pair of shorts and a tank top, and combed through her long, thick mass of wet, black curls. Today was going to be an all natural day.

She started down the stairs, noting that Eli's bedroom door was still closed, indicating he was sleeping uncharacteristically later than usual. She stopped in the living room and opened the plantation shutters only to catch sight of a figure sitting in a lawn chair by the pond; his back toward the house.

"Oh," Delilah said aloud. "He's not sleeping, he's fishing."

She slipped her gardening Crocs on at the back door, and then traipsed across the lawn and driveway. With some effort, she climbed over the metal gate to the pasture, and called out Eli's name. There was no response. She kept walking, laughing at the ball cap he was wearing. She had never seen him in a ball cap. He'd always worn a cowboy hat when doing chores around the ranch.

As she got closer, she called Eli's name again, adding that she felt much better, and that the little pill he'd given her really worked. She thought it was peculiar that he hadn't responded or moved. At all.

"Eli?" she said placing a hand on his shoulder as she reached him.

The chair, and the man toppled over in slow motion, and Delilah screamed at the sight of a small, blackened hole in his forehead.

She ran back to the house, stumbling a couple times, and shouting "Oh shit!" every few seconds. She was crying by the time she reached the back steps, and ran blindly into Eli who was coming out the back door.

"There's a, a dead man fishing at the, the," she stammered, pointing a shaking finger toward the pond. "The pond."

"What?" Eli said, clearly confused.

"There's a man at the pond," she said an octave higher, "with a fishing pole. He's . . . he's dead."

Eli, stunned into brief silence, glanced quickly in the direction of the pond, and then back at Delilah. "Are you sure he's dead?" he asked.

Delilah's eyes went wide. "Pretty sure. I mean, the bullet hole in his head is pretty much a dead giveaway. No pun intended."

"You better call Charlie," Eli said calmly. "And STAY. IN. The house."

An hour later, Delilah watched from the living room window as the man's body was hoisted onto a gurney, and rolled into the ambulance. There was an officer at the pond where the deceased had been sitting on his nylon lawn chair, and two officers combing the pasture for evidence. The coroner had just left, and the sheriff, Eli and Gus were moving toward the back door of the house.

Delilah scurried to the kitchen to intercept them.

"Are you alright?" Eli asked softly, the moment he saw Delilah.

"No!" she answered, practically hysterical. "This is awful! Just . . . awful."

She began crying again, and Eli embraced her. "That could've been me. Or you! Or Gus!" she shrieked, sobbing.

A wave of determination swept over Delilah and she suddenly became quite resolved. She gently pulled away from Eli, and wiped the tears from her cheeks. "That Murray guy did this, Charlie!" she said obstinately.

"No, Murray didn't do this?" Charlie said, just as determined.

"How can you be sure?" Delilah argued.

"Because the dead guy is Murray," Eli said.

Delilah stood completely paralyzed, replaying over and over in her mind what she'd just heard. It finally occurred to her that she needed to take a breath before she passed out. "Well," she said, totally at a loss for words. "I didn't see that coming."

And then comprehension gave her a good, strong slap in the face. "That means . . . the killer's still out there."

"Yeah," Charlie said. "And we have to consider other options."

Charlie turned and stepped toward the back door. "I'll be in touch. I hope you're not planning on pulling another disappearing act, Eli" he said contentiously. "And Delilah, it might be prudent for you to let Herbert know what's going on."

"Why does my attorney need to know?" Delilah began, chasing after Charlie. "Wait just a minute, Charlie. You don't honestly think I had anything to do with this, do you?"

"I don't know what to think anymore," Charlie replied, walking to his car.

Delilah phoned Herbert and advised him she may be a suspect in the murder of Murray Rockford, and though she had not been officially charged, the sheriff had recommended she contact her lawyer.

"Oh, by the way," Delilah continued with little emotion. "Eli's back in town."

Herbert suggested that he pay a visit to the ranch the following day, thereby killing two birds with one stone; interviewing Delilah, and taking care of Eli's legal matters. He indicated his arrival would be sometime in the afternoon as he had appointments in the morning.

Delilah then called, and conveyed the situation to Karon, who was mortified.

The following morning, just after the breakfast dishes had been washed, Charlie contacted Delilah and requested she come to his office, alone. Delilah agreed, told Eli she was going to town for groceries, and then drove to Chandler.

At the station, Delilah was ushered into Charlie's office.

"I wanted to visit with you without Eli being present," Charlie said, as he gestured toward a chair for her to sit in. He closed his office door, sat down at his desk, and continued. "How involved are you with Eli?"

Delilah gave a small but perceptible shake of her head, and coupled with the confused look on her face, Charlie pressed on.

"Are you sleeping with him?" Charlie said, succinctly.

"I beg your pardon," Delilah said.

"I'm asking this question for a very specific reason," Charlie said. "Could you testify, in court, that Eli didn't leave the house night before last?"

She thought about the massive dose of Nyquil and the little pill Eli had given her. "Look," she said. "I was sick. I took Nyquil, and went to bed about 9:00. King Kong could have come calling, and I would never have known. I have no idea what Eli did after I went to bed. But I really don't believe he killed Murray."

"I find that I'm in a difficult spot here, Delilah," Charlie pressed on with caution. "You're either in the best of hands, or the worst of hands. If Eli is innocent, then he's going to take care of you. If he's guilty, then he's going to take care of you . . . in a different way. There are so many unanswered questions. For instance, it's odd that Murray winds up dead within 48 hours of Eli's return. And that's another odd thing, Eli was gone during the time of the incidents; or was he? Was it Murray, or someone setting up Murray?"

"You know something else that's odd?" Delilah said mockingly. "I can't think of a single motive Eli would have for getting rid of me, can you? And something else, don't you think it's strange that Murray's dead body was left in a nylon lawn chair beside my pond? I mean, if I had killed him I certainly would not have staged his body that way on my own property. And I'm pretty sure Eli's smarter than that, too."

"Yeah," Charlie said with a hint of a grin. "That is a bit of a mystery. And how did you know Murray had been shot somewhere else?"

"I caught enough of the conversations to figure that out, Charlie," she said.

Mean while, back at the ranch . . . Eli was in the kitchen preparing a pot of coffee, while a fidgeting Herbert sat in the living room, pulling documents from his briefcase and spreading them on the coffee table.

"As I'm sure you recall," Herbert said as Eli sat a cup of coffee on the end table next to Herbert, and then took a seat in the wing back chair close by. "You named Nettie as the beneficiary to your estate with no secondary recipient. With Nettie's death it has become necessary for you to revise your will. I hope you have been giving this some consideration."

Eli nodded. "I want Delilah to have it," he said.

Herbert forced back a smile and adjusted his bow tie. "I had no idea the two of you were that close," he said.

"Get your mind out of the gutter, Herbert," Eli cautioned. "Delilah's the closest thing to family I have."

"I see," Herbert pressed. "She's like a sister."

Eli laughed. "No, not exactly. It's . . . complicated."

"So you ARE in love with her," Herbert said passively pushing his glasses up the bridge of his nose.

Eli studied Herbert a moment. Herbert was, after all, his attorney. But this was a very personal matter; one he'd shared only with Nettie. Eli drew in a deep breath, and said, "I've loved Delilah since the first moment I saw her over thirty years ago. No distance of place or lapse of time has changed that. It's clear what forces brought us back together, but unclear what direction we're going. The only thing you need to be concerned with is the legalities."

"Very well," Herbert said, making notes. "And she's to have everything; all of the stocks, the insurance, the condos in Brazil and Morocco?"

"Everything," Eli conferred.

"And is she to be made aware of this development?" Herbert asked.

"I'll tell her when the time's right," Eli answered stoically. His mood shifted, and he chuckled. "Delilah still thinks I'm some poor, struggling geologist who flits around the world hunting rocks. I think it best she continues believing that for as long as possible."

It wasn't long before Delilah sat in the living room with Eli and Herbert, going over her account of the events leading up to and including her discovery of Murray's dead body. She stuck to the simple facts, and didn't elaborate. She excluded, for example, Eli's insistence she go to bed early, and failed to mention the little pill he had given her, as well as his mysterious telephone conversation that afternoon.

Satisfied that he had the facts he needed, Herbert bid goodbye to Delilah and Eli, assuring the former that she had nothing to worry about.

That evening, as Delilah and Eli were supping at the kitchen table, there was a knock on the back door.

"Oh, you're still here," Karon said tersely to Eli as she sauntered in the kitchen.

"And hello to you, too, Karon," Eli replied with a grin.

"Have you eaten?" Delilah asked. "There's plenty."

Karon made a bee line for the stove, and raised the lid on the pot of spaghetti and meatballs. "I just came out to check on you," Karon said as she pulled a plate from the cupboard. She went back to the stove where she dished up a mountain of pasta.

"Is your cell phone dead?" Karon asked, sitting down at the table. "I tried to call, but it went straight to voice mail."

"Must be," Delilah said.

Karon shot Eli the evil eye between bites of food. Finally, Eli addressed her with an air of playfulness.

"Karon," he said. "I sense you want to say something to me."

"She thinks you're a spy," Delilah offered nonchalantly.

For a split second Eli had the look of a little boy caught with his hand in the cookie jar. But just as quickly his expression turned quite serious, as did Karon's.

"Where did you slink off to so secret like?" Karon asked in a stare down with Eli.

"If I told you, I'd have to kill you," he replied without a blink. "I must say, it's extraordinarily astute of you, Karon. But the truth is . . . I've been out of the spy business for about three years now." The signature, crooked, mischievous smile stretched across Eli's face.

"Oh, no you didn't," Karon proclaimed with a wagging finger, and a jerk of the head. "I know when I'm being patronized. You can't throw me off track just by agreein' with me."

Delilah and Eli burst into laughter.

"Oh, Karon!" Eli said at last, his voice cracking with chuckles. "I'm a geologist; working for the USGS on a classified project in the Canary Islands. That's all I can tell you. And that was too much."

This explanation apparently appeased Karon's curiosity, because her mood lightened, and she warmed to Eli. Delilah, however, was not so easily swayed. She had one question; one question she ultimately opted not to ask. What was the United States Geological Survey doing an ocean away in the Canary Islands?

Two days passed in which it was business as usual on the ranch. The horses were tended to, the pastures and lawns were maintained, and Eli and Delilah interacted with close, albeit controlled, pleasantries.

On more than one occasion Delilah caught Eli staring at her intently. She would smile at him. He would return the smile, and then make some goofy remark that produced a chuckle from both of them.

Late Friday afternoon, as they finished their chores, Delilah asked Eli if there had been any mail, to which he responded that he hadn't checked the mail that day.

Delilah drove the pickup down to the road, and gathered the mail from the box, along with a package wrapped in plain, brown paper, that had been addressed to her, and placed on the ground beneath the mail box.

When Delilah entered the back door of the house, she sat the package on the kitchen table, and sorted through the remaining pieces of mail. As her attention was directed back to the package, Eli entered the room.

"Where did you get that package?" he asked suspiciously.

"It was with the mail," she answered, as she reached to open it.

"Don't touch it!" Eli shouted, racing toward her. "It could be a bomb."

Chapter 11

Exes Are Forever

"It's not a bomb," Delilah said. "It's from my parents. What's the date today?"

"May 30th," Eli replied.

"Oh my gosh! My birthday is tomorrow," she said tearing the package open. "I completely forgot."

She extracted a card from the box, and read the short message to herself. "Happy Birthday - Hannah."

"Oh, Mother," Delilah said with a laugh, handing the card to Eli. "She's still angry with me for living on a ranch in Oklahoma; Aunt Nettie's ranch."

"She doesn't approve," Eli stated after reading the note.

"She doesn't approve," Delilah agreed. "In Hannah Beauregard's world, I'm advantageously married to a grotesquely rich man, living in a grandiose mansion in Atlanta, and hosting extravagant dinner parties for snooty dignitaries.

That would impress her contemporaries far more than my living alone on a two bit ranch in Oklahoma, wallowing in horse poo."

After extracting a Gucci handbag, and a pair of 14 karat gold, button earrings from the box, Delilah called her parents and thanked them. The conversation with her mother was short; the conversation with Buford, longer.

The following morning at breakfast, Eli informed Delilah that he was taking her to Stillwater to celebrate her birthday.

Delilah perked up at the suggestion. "That's great," she said enthusiastically. "I've been thinking about painting the living room. And I may even pull up that awful carpet, and redo the hardwood floors. Maybe we can get paint while we're there."

This thought had been lurking in the back of Delilah's mind for weeks. Now, more than ever, she needed a diversion from the mess that had become her life.

She promptly went upstairs and changed into her best pair of blue jeans, a light-weight, royal blue sweater, and sandals. When she returned downstairs, she was met by Eli, who had also changed into starched jeans, a crisp white, short sleeved shirt, and shiny alligator-skin cowboy boots.

Delilah grinned as she looked him up and down.

"What?" Eli asked.

"I'm just so accustomed to seeing you in work jeans and T-shirts. You clean up nicely," she said.

Eli laughed. "The same could be said about you. Are you ready?"

After having lunch at Eskimo Joes, Eli suggested they catch a matinee.

"Well," Delilah said. "Is there anything in particular you want to see?"

"It's your birthday," he replied. "You choose. As long as it's not animated or about vampires, I'm good."

Delilah laughed. "Okay, but you realize you just cut our choices in half."

A stop at the home improvement chain store was in order after the movie, and before the trip back home. Once inside, Delilah made a bee line straight for the power tools. She ooed and awed over several items, and actually hugged the cordless nail gun. Eventually, she tore herself away from them, and went to the paint department.

She poured over the paint color selections, picked out her paint and primer, and watched carefully as the assistant mixed it. Meanwhile, Eli browsed in other parts of the store.

Finally catching up to Eli, Delilah announced that she was not only going to paint the living room, but the dining room as well, and she planned on pulling the carpet up in both rooms.

"Since we have the pickup," Delilah reasoned. "We may as well get the quarter round for the base boards, don't you think?"

"Okay," Eli said. "How much do you need?"

"Well, let's see. The living room is 14 by 20," Delilah said, calculating in the empty space above Eli's right shoulder. "So, 68 feet for the living room, and 14 by 12 in the dining room is . . . 52 feet. Better get 120 feet, half-inch wide."

"Yeah, but there's . . . 22 feet of door space you don't need," Eli offered after a little calculating of his own."

"Which is exactly the allowance I need for error," Delilah said happily.

Delilah checked out, paying for her paint, supplies, and quarter round, and met Eli at the pickup, where he loaded the goods with the help of an assistant.

"I caught a glimpse of two DeWalt boxes in the back of the pickup," Delilah said as they made their way north on Perkins Road. "What did you get?"

"I got your birthday present," he answered.

"What?" she said shocked.

"Didn't you ask your parents for a double-bevel, compound miter saw for Christmas?" he asked with a sly grin.

"Well, yes," she answered, recalling that she had mentioned this in passing when they were in Arkansas weeks ago. "But . . ."

"Oh," he said, nodding his head in comprehension. "Power tools aren't a good gift to give a woman."

"What, are you kidding?" Delilah said. "I mean, most women would probably give you the silent treatment for days over a gift like that, but I love power tools."

He laughed. "Good. Because I got you that cordless nail gun you were drooling over, too."

Silence fell in the pickup cab. Delilah didn't know what to say. She didn't feel right accepting gifts of this magnitude from Eli. He'd spent a lot of money, and she felt guilty.

Finally Delilah spoke. "Eli, I don't want you to think I'm not appreciative. I am. I'm just so overwhelmed. You paid for the gate at the ranch. That had to be a pretty penny. I don't think it's fair that you spend your hard earned money on me."

"Look," he said quickly. "If you're too uncomfortable accepting the tools as a personal gift, then just look at it as tools that have been purchased for the ranch. You NEED a miter saw, and that cordless nail gun is going to come in handy when we install the 120 feet of quarter round you just bought."

Delilah smiled. "Okay, but I owe you," she said.

"No you don't," Eli contradicted. "And where did you develop such a liking for power tools, anyway?"

Delilah shook her head and sighed. Once again the master of diversion had changed the subject. "Dooby," she answered. "He's a carpenter, slash engineer, slash genius, when it comes to building things. We collaborated on a number of projects when I had my Interior Design business. He's big on the Chinese proverb, 'give a man a fish and you feed him for a day, teach a man to fish and you feed him for a lifetime.' Only in my case it was more like, 'build for Delilah and you're building for a lifetime, teach Delilah to build and enjoy peaceful afternoons fishing.'"

Eli roared with laughter.

It was nearly 7:00 by the time they rolled into Cushing. Eli asked Delilah if she was hungry, and she replied that she was. Insisting that she would do no more cooking on her birthday, Eli pulled into Naifeh's.

After they had eaten, and the plates were placed at the edge of the table for the wait staff to remove, something over Delilah's left shoulder caught Eli's attention.

"Oh, no," he groaned, as he slipped lower in his seat. "This can't be happening."

With a jerk of her head, Delilah looked over her shoulder. Walking at a fast pace toward them was a woman wearing a smirk. She was average height, with a slender build, and impeccable taste in clothing. Her short, bob haircut was light brown with blonde highlights, and her eyes were brown. Delilah guessed her to be in her late twenties to early thirties.

"Eli," the woman said as she reached the table. "I didn't know you were back in town."

Eli fought the urge to grimace, and with a nod, said, "Nicole."

Nicole shot a contemptuous glare at Delilah, and then looked back at Eli. "How long have you been back? And who is this lovely creature?" she asked sarcastically. "New girlfriend?"

"No!" Eli practically shouted. Composing himself, Eli continued. "Nicole this is Delilah. Delilah, Nicole."

Delilah was taken aback by Eli's denial; not so much that he'd done it, but more the *way* he'd done it. She hesitated a moment, then extended her hand. "Pleased to meet you," Delilah said politely.

Nicole scowled and turned her attention back to Eli. "So, if she's not your girlfriend, then who is she?" she asked with an acrid hiss.

Delilah had endured the ill-mannered woman all she could. "Oh, I'm not his girlfriend, hun," Delilah said sweetly. "He just lives with me on my ranch."

Nicole smiled deviously. "Is that right, HUN. Well, lover boy, this one is a lot older than what you're accustomed to." She looked back at Delilah. "And plumper," she added.

Eli was clearly irritated as they walked out the door of the restaurant, and headed toward the pickup.

"Why do women have to be so competitive?" he asked.

"I think that's kind of a broad generalization," Delilah offered. "And if I remember correctly she was the one who called me fat. Of course my memory could be slipping. I am, after all, old."

This comment failed to amuse, so Delilah took a different approach. "Look, I'm sorry if I messed things up for you," she said regretfully.

"What?" Eli said, completely shocked, as he unlocked Delilah's door, and then opened it for her.

"You don't understand," he continued, climbing into the pickup and starting it. "She is trouble; with a capital T. I dated her a few years back. Mind you, only briefly. But she has a real problem letting go. She's of the mind that once she's had you, no one else can. You know what I mean? She could cause a lot of problems for you; like you don't have enough already.

"Oh, man," he groaned. "I thought she moved away to Kalamazoo, or Timbuktu. Or maybe she'd been swallowed up by a huge sink hole, or taken out by a bolt of lightning, or abducted by aliens."

"Yeah," Delilah said bleakly. "I think you just crossed over into the realm of wishful thinking." Delilah decided to switch gears. "Okay, maybe she's mellowed," she offered.

Eli shot Delilah a look of complete incredulity. "Really?"

"I just joined you in that realm, didn't I?" she said.

The drive home was spent with Delilah alternating between thanking Eli for a wonderful day, and apologizing for saying too much to Nicole. All the while Eli was checking the rearview mirror every five seconds.

Given some thought, it occurred to Delilah that she had never seen Eli this flustered. He always seemed so cool, calm and collected, even fearless. He was genuinely frightened of this woman. On one hand it was marginally humorous, on the other hand, slightly disturbing.

Sunday passed, free of threats from old adversaries or new, and just after breakfast

Monday morning, Charlie came knocking with his deputy in tow.

Delilah invited them in the house and poured them a cup of coffee. She then joined Eli, Gus, and the two officials at the kitchen table.

"So, do you have any news?" Delilah asked anxiously.

"Well," Charlie began. "I'll get right to it. Looks like Murray was shot with a .45 Ruger. Nettie had a .45 Ruger, didn't she?"

Delilah's heart sank. "Yeah," she answered slowly. "It's in the gun cabinet in the living room."

She stood to fetch it, but Charlie asked her to let the deputy get it. She nodded, and the deputy exited the room.

"There's something you need to know, Charlie," Eli interjected. He took a deep breath and continued. "Nicole met Delilah Saturday night."

There was a short pause in which Charlie's expression went from vacant to exasperated. "Oh, shit!" he said. "You're kidding, right? I thought she moved to Amarillo or Chicago, or maybe she'd been caught in a herd of stampeding buffalo, or someone dropped a house on her."

Delilah forced back a grin.

"Well, did you tell her Delilah was your sister?" Charlie asked Eli.

"She knows I don't have family," Eli said. "Besides, Delilah let it slip that I was living on the ranch with her."

Charlie shook his head and growled. He glared at Eli. "Oh, shit!"

Delilah watched the two men in a stare down for a moment, and then she spoke up. "I wish someone would tell me why there's so much animosity between the two of you."

"Which version do you want?" Charlie said.

The deputy entered the room holding the gun in his gloved hand. "It's been fired recently, Charlie," he said.

Charlie looked anxiously at Delilah. "Well, Dave," he said with a heavy sigh. "I guess you better get the cuffs out."

"You don't need to cuff me, Charlie," Delilah said. "I'll go with you willingly, but not until I've brushed my hair, and put lipstick on."

The three men looked quizzically at Delilah.

"The last mug shot I had taken was awful. That's not going to happen again," she said.

"Not taking you in, Delilah," Charlie said with a chuckle. "We're taking Eli."

"What?" Delilah and Eli said in unison.

Two hours later, Delilah sat in Charlie's office waiting for the interrogation to conclude. When Charlie entered the room and sat at his desk, Delilah asked if she and Eli could go home.

"Not yet," Charlie said as he made a note. "Can I get you anything?"

"No," she answered. "But you can tell me why you and Eli despise each other so much."

"Despise is a little strong," Charlie said. He studied Delilah a moment.

"For starters," he began. "Eli and I were never the best of friends. We were highly competitive in high school. And then there were a few incidences when he came home from college. I was new on the police force, and he was . . . rowdy. He was resentful of my authoritative position."

"One question before you continue, Charlie," Delilah said quickly. "And be honest. Did you take advantage of your position where Eli was concerned?"

He studied her again, and then answered with some hesitation. "Might have. But then he settled down some, and I never saw him except in passing. Then a few years back, when he was home from one of his world jaunts, I happened to see him out with Nicole. We'd had plenty of experience with her in the past, so I cautioned Eli about the trouble he was getting into."

"He didn't believe you?" Delilah asked.

"It wasn't that," he answered. "I think it was more that he didn't appreciate the interference. I think he thought at the time, and based on our history, that my intentions were vindictively based. That is until she went ballistic on him and destroyed some of his property. Then she made the mistake of threatening Nettie."

"What?" Delilah gasped.

"Oh, yeah," Charlie said with a laugh. "You can just imagine how well that went over. It's a wonder Nettie didn't kill her. For as long as I live, I'll never forget the things Nettie suggested be done with that woman. Hard to believe such horrible thoughts could come from such a nice old woman." He paused in deep thought. "Was she ever in combat?"

Delilah laughed. "I don't think so."

"Well," Charlie continued. "The conclusion to that story is, Eli started seeing my sister about a year after his disastrous encounter with Nicole, and it resulted in a pretty bad accident at Nicole's hand."

Delilah gasped.

"She's alright," Charlie assured her. "But suffice it to say, Brenda stopped seeing Eli." There was a long stretch of silence in which Charlie made a few more notes.

"Charlie?" Delilah finally said in a low voice. "Do you believe Eli shot Murray?"

Again, there was an extended moment of contemplation for Charlie. "I don't want to believe it," he said sincerely. "But I'm one hundred percent certain he's capable."

Delilah dropped the subject like a hot potato. A frightening chill coursed through her. She didn't want to know what Eli was capable of, or why. Maybe Karon had it right. Maybe he was a spy.

The overwhelming tension between Delilah and Eli made for little conversation as they drove back to the ranch. Even though Charlie had concluded that the lack of evidence prevented them from locking Eli up, the investigation was still ongoing. Once they were inside the house and settled on the sofa in the living room, Eli took a stab at breaking down the wall between them.

"Charlie told you, didn't he?" he asked.

"Yes," Delilah answered softly, "at least from his perspective."

After repeating what Charlie had told her, Eli concurred that it was a relatively accurate account of events.

"You must think I'm a real jerk," he said.

"No," Delilah said softly. "At some point in our lives we've all made bad choices. And some bad choices stay with us longer than others; Nicole being a prime example of that. But that doesn't make us rotten or evil. I believe it's what follows that counts."

Eli smiled slightly. "Sounds like something Nettie would say," he said.

"Nettie DID say that," Delilah concurred. She smiled. "Well, maybe not in those exact words. But the message was the same. I think Nettie's exact words were, 'Hell, everybody screws up. It don't make 'em the devil.'"

With great emotion, Eli gently touched the back of his hand to Delilah's cheek. Their eyes met, and there was a fleeting moment when their souls had opened up to each other. Then, just as quickly, and with a slight shake of his head, Eli appeared to think better of any attempts to pursue the matter any further.

"Let's paint," he said, standing.

The remainder of the day was spent clearing the living room and dining room of clutter, and small furniture. Removing pictures and art from the walls and placing it on the floor in the entry hall, stacked vertically against the wall.

"There's a Renoir under this drawing," Delilah indicated as she pulled Abigail's drawing from the wall above the fireplace.

Eli shot her a disbelieving look.

"I'll show you when we're through painting," Delilah promised, and she added it to the stack in the entry hall.

After the antique armoire was emptied of the television and Bose stereo, it joined the sofa in the middle of the living room. Nettie's old, oak desk was a bit more of a challenge. It required the removal of the side drawers. Delilah suggested that the lap drawer stay in the desk, as it had a tendency to get stuck. Even with the drawers absent, it was difficult to maneuver the beast.

The sideboard in the dining room was moved to the kitchen, and the built-in, corner china cabinet was emptied of dishes.

"Are you sure you don't want to pull up the carpet BEFORE we paint?" Eli asked. "It just seems like it would be easier without the carpet."

"You've never seen me paint," Delilah said. "Trust me, we want the hardwoods covered."

The nail holes were filled, and the trim around the windows and doors was caulked. Plastic sheets were draped over the furniture left in the rooms. It was 9:30. Delilah and Eli were pooped.

A light rain was falling, the following morning, and during breakfast Gus offered his assistance with the painting project, since there was little he could do outdoors.

"Boy," Gus said after they had sanded the rough spots and wiped down all the surfaces. "You take thith painting thing theriouthly."

"Eighty percent of a good paint job is preparation," Delilah said.

"I'll try to remember that," Gus said with a chuckle. "What now?"

"Let's roll," Delilah said playfully rubbing her hands together. "I'll cut in, you roll behind me."

"You don't want to mask it off?" Eli asked.

"Don't need to," Delilah said with a wink and a grin.

By 8:00 that evening, the second coat of primer was drying on all the ceilings, walls, and trim. And Delilah? She was a spotted mess. It was in her hair, up her nose, under her fingernails, and somehow she'd even managed to get some on her feet which had been in shoes all day.

"I told you," she said, as Eli and Gus looked her up and down, shaking their heads.

"I've never theen anyone paint like that," Gus said.

"Dooby can paint an entire house and never get a drop of paint on him," she said. "I'm sorry, but there's just something wrong with that. And look at the two of you; scarcely any paint at all on either of you."

Delilah felt a contentment that had been absent for days, possibly even weeks. She had channeled her energy into creative 'ideas' instead of 'things' that were happening. It seemed when her mind was in 'idea' mode, decisiveness concerning 'things' came quicker and easier.

Though it never rained the next day, it threatened to. So, once again, Gus lent his services to the job inside the house. By the end of the day, the painting was complete, with the exception of the baseboards which would be done after the floors were finished.

Eli and Delilah removed the carpet the day after, and much to Delilah's absolute delight, the oak floors were in excellent condition, and only needed to be cleaned well, which she did once all the staples were removed.

The following day they were nailing the primed quarter round into the baseboards. "I love this cordless nail gun!" Delilah exclaimed as she shot one nail after another into the trim. "Now that's what I'm talkin' about. This is almost as much fun as driving Carlotta. I am so glad you bought this, Eli."

"I told you," Eli said with a gratified smile. "It's a shame you can't shoot a pistol as well as you shoot that nail gun."

Delilah laughed. "That's funny. And if it weren't true I'd be inclined to be offended. Why do you suppose the nail gun's easier?"

"Because your target is closer," Eli said.

The landline rang, and amongst the laughter Delilah asked Eli to answer it, as she stood and placed the nail gun on top the plastic covering the desk.

"Hey, Charlie," Eli said in a carefree tone Delilah had never heard him use with Charlie.

Eli shot a portentous glance at Delilah. Immediately, the reality that she had so efficaciously abandoned for the past few days was back and haunting her again.

"Today?" Eli asked. There was a pause, and then Eli said, "I'll head that way."

"What?" Delilah asked, once Eli hung up the phone.

Eli rubbed his chin, and looked nervous. "Delilah," he said almost in a panic. "Nettie used to keep a journal. Have you seen it? Do you know where it is?"

"I know what you're talking about," she replied, visibly shaken. "But I haven't seen it."

Eli shook his head, and his demeanor instantly calmed. "Okay," he said. "Charlie's asked me to come to his office."

"You want me to go with you?" Delilah urged.

"No," Eli answered. He glanced around the room. "Uh, look, why don't you knock off until I get back?"

"Why?" she asked.

"Because I'd rather be here when you're using the tools," he said.

Delilah put her hand on her hip to object.

"Please?" Eli pleaded.

"Okay," she capitulated.

"See if you can locate the journal," he said. He kissed her forehead, and told her he'd be back as soon as possible.

Delilah sat on the arm of the sofa for a long stretch contemplating where the journal could be. She didn't recall seeing it in any of the things that were moved to the barn or apartment. It wasn't in any of Nettie's things that stayed in the house.

She looked over at the desk. Her eyes lit on the lap drawer; the lap drawer that was always sticking. With a burst of inspiration, she pulled the plastic cover away from the front of the desk, and tugged on the drawer. There was definitely something catching the drawer. She gave a forceful tug, and pulled the drawer completely out. To her utter astonishment, the journal fell to the floor.

She grabbed the journal, sat down on the sofa, and began scanning the entries. At first they were a representation of Nettie's wit and wisdom. Delilah's fingers raced through the text. She made a mental note to come back and read it again when she had more time. She flipped frantically through the pages until the entries suddenly became more troubling.

Eli had been part of a team that had discovered a large deposit of oil on the land. Nettie had refused to drill. Most shocking of all, were the notations made just weeks before her death, in which she confessed she didn't know who to trust. And the last entry was a reference to a document that would incriminate the one who was plotting to get the ranch.

Delilah jumped as the landline rang again.

"Is your cell phone dead?" Karon asked. "I called but didn't get an answer."

"It's in my purse upstairs," Delilah said. "Sorry, I didn't hear it.

"Listen, Karon," Delilah said nervously. "I've found something of Nettie's that . . ." Delilah was fighting back tears. She took a deep breath and continued. "Something that explains why there's been such an effort to get me off the ranch. And I think I may know who's behind it, but I can't be certain. I have to find the documents that prove it. They're somewhere here in the house."

After a moment's silence, Karon said, "maybe I should come out there and help you."

"No," Delilah said. "But thanks for the offer."

Delilah hung up, and thoroughly combed through all the documents in the drawers that had been removed from the desk. Finding nothing, she searched the closet under the stairs, and then the hall closets upstairs. Still having no luck finding the documentation, she returned to the living room, and plopped down on the sofa.

"Think, Delilah. Think," she told herself. She half-heartedly looked around the room until her eyes fell upon the spot where a child's drawing once hung. And then she remembered.

"You know, Delilah," Aunt Nettie had said. "It's always important not to take things at face value. So often people and things aren't what they appear to be. For instance," she continued, making a dramatic gesture toward the child art on the wall. "What do you think of this lovely drawing Abigail sent me when she was five years old?"

"I like it. It reminds me of when Abigail had a delightfully fun innocence," Delilah replied.

"Now what do you think of it?" Nettie said as she magically pulled the drawing out of the frame, revealing something else behind it.

"Aunt Nettie, is that,"

"Yes dear, it's a Renoir."

Delilah gasped, and jumped to her feet. She raced to the entry hall and flipped through the art that had been moved out of the living room and dining room. She wrenched the frame and its contents from the stack, and found the miniscule button at the lower left corner of the frame. She pushed it. Again, she was amazed when the drawing and two other pieces of paper fell from the bottom.

She returned to the sofa, and began reading. Her heart sank when she reached the bottom of the first page. Eli was to inherit the ranch in the event of Delilah's death, or in the event she forfeited her inheritance. Her hands began to shake, and she could feel her heart pounding in her chest. Tears pooled in her eyes as she continued reading the second page intently.

Then, without notice, the document was wrenched out of her trembling hands. She jumped with fright, and turned with a jerk to see who was behind her.

"So now you know," he said, standing with the document in one hand, and a .45 caliber, Glock G37 in the other hand,

"I trusted you," she said, tears streaming down her cheeks. "Aunt Nettie trusted you."

Chapter 12

It's Not Who You Think

"I know," Herbert said, with a taunting kindness. Though the attorney was still a fidgeting mess, the kindness and warmth in his eyes was gone. A maniacal glint had taken up residency there. In one hand he held the truth, in the other, the means to eliminate the only other living person who knew the truth. And he was pointing the gun at Delilah's chest.

Delilah's mind was slowly making the shift from victim to survivor. She stood slowly, and considered her options; the door from the living room to the dining room, where she could possibly escape through the French doors onto the screened porch, or the door into the entry hall, which was blocked by Herbert. The distance to each was about the same. She thought if she could keep him talking she might be able to inch her way into a more advantages position.

"Was it you all along?" she asked, taking a single step toward the dining room.

"Murray was in on it," he answered. "I told him I could get the property, and promised him a substantial cut if he helped. He did all the grunt work; wrote the notes, sabotaged the propane tank, ran the wire in the barn."

"Rigged the brakes on the pickup?" Delilah said, taking another fluid step.

"No," Herbert said with a braggadocios air. "I did that, the day I brought you the check. That was the day I took the gun, too. I rigged the brakes, and then slipped into the house and got the gun. I'd just come out of the house when Gus pulled up. He of course thought you had given me the gate code."

"How DID you get in the gate?"

"Ah. I had Murray sit in that thicket of sand plum trees across the road with a pair of binoculars, and wait for one of you to key the number into the pad."

Delilah processed this information a moment "And when did you return the gun?" she finally asked.

"The day I was here about Eli's will. While he was in the kitchen making coffee, I just slipped it right back into the gun cabinet."

Delilah's mind was racing with questions she wanted answered, while at the same time attempting to stay focused on survival. She made another move.

"Well, it's perfectly understandable why you never showed me the documents you're holding. You are our proxy. Only, Aunt Nettie found out you'd made a deal with the oil company, and she was in the process of changing that. Which means you would have lost control of the property."

"Very good, Delilah," he said condescendingly.

Delilah felt a lump rise in her throat. She hesitated before asking the next question because she wasn't altogether certain she wanted the answer. She took a deep breath and another step closer to the dining room door.

"Did you kill Aunt Nettie?" she blurted out. "Did you have Murray kill her?"

"No. Fortunately she died of natural causes," he said smugly.

This remark seemed to transform Delilah's fear to rage, and she felt the heat of her anger in her face. The instant rush of adrenaline inspired her to charge around the armoire, bringing her closer to the door, and closer to Herbert.

"FORTUNATELY?" she shouted.

Herbert reacted to the sudden move and outburst by stepping further into the room and away from the door to the entry hall. His back was now toward the front windows, and Delilah was just a few steps from the dining room door. He extended the gun and told her not to move.

Delilah held up her hands, and continued with her questioning. "So, the way I have it figured, Murray was going to kill me with Nettie's gun, and then you would frame Eli for the murder."

"Brilliant plan really," Herbert said. "With both of you out of the way, I have control."

"So why kill Murray?"

"That idiot was getting sloppy," Herbert said, clearly agitated. "Then he decided he wanted

277

a bigger cut, and threatened to go to the police if I didn't agree. I couldn't let him screw that up."

At that moment Delilah saw movement outside the window behind Herbert. Her heart sank. It was Karon. When Karon saw the gun in Herbert's hand her eyes bugged out and she began jerking and dancing about. If she'd been forty pounds thinner and white, she'd have looked very much like Barney Fife in a state of panic.

Delilah took another step closer to the dining room door, prompting Herbert to move further into the room, and less likely to see what was going on outside.

"Come on," Herbert said with a wave of the gun. "Let's go."

"Go?" Delilah said. "I'm not going anywhere. If you're going to kill me, you'll have to do it here."

Then several things happened in rapid succession. The house phone, which sat on the arm of the sofa, and just about half way between Delilah and Herbert, rang. They both lunged for it. Herbert reached it first, and as he let go of the documents, he took hold of the phone and yanked it, pulling the cord from the wall. Delilah reached for the gun in Herbert's other hand. And Herbert smacked Delilah across the face with the phone.

She stumbled a couple steps backward, while Herbert dropped the phone and started toward her. He grabbed the front of her blouse and pulled her towards him as she pulled back. The buttons on the blouse popped, and a piece of the fabric was ripped away from the garment.

Delilah stumbled backward again. Instinctually, she reached for the desk to steady herself and her hand rested right beside the nail gun.

In one swift, fluid move, Delilah grasped the nail gun and switched the safety off. She swung it forward, shooting off a round as she did so. The first nail missed Herbert's arm by inches, and sailed across the room, but she nailed the second shot right in Herbert's left shoulder.

As Herbert stumbled backward with the force and pain of the shot, Delilah fired off shot number three, quite by accident, which miraculously hit the gun in Herbert's hand, and sent it sailing across the room and under a drop cloth.

She dropped the nail gun, and rushed toward him. She grabbed him by both shoulders, pushing the nail in a little deeper, and simultaneously raised her knee forcefully to make contact with his groin.

The man went down screaming in agony. Delilah scanned the room in search of the gun. She couldn't see it. She needed something to knock him out; something with weight. She grabbed the closest thing available; a full gallon of paint.

Still wailing, Herbert made an effort to stand.

"Herbert, just stay down," she warned.

He growled fiercely and began crawling toward her.

"You idiot," Delilah said as Herbert crawled ever closer. "All right, I did warn you."

And with that, she swung the can of paint with all her might, and it caught him across the jaw. There was a loud pop and crunching sound, and Herbert was laid out cold.

Seconds later, Karon was running in the back door and down the hall, screaming, "Sweet Jesus." She slid to a stop at the living room door, and looked down at Herbert.

"Is he out?" she asked.

Delilah nodded.

"Sweet Jesus! You shot him with a nail gun. I couldn't believe it."

"Was that you calling on the phone?"

"Yeah," Karon said, panting. "I didn't know what to do. I figured you needed a diversion. And girl, you are bleeding like a stuck pig."

"Hand me your phone," Delilah said, patting her cheek with a trembling hand. And then her entire body was shaking uncontrollably.

"They're on their way, honey," Karon said softly. "I called the sheriff before I called you."

She took hold of Delilah's arm and guided her to the sofa. Delilah sat. Karon turned to find a blanket.

"Please don't leave me!" Delilah cried out, her voice cracking with sobs.

Karon sat down on the sofa, took Delilah in her arms, and began gently rocking her. "I ain't gonna leave ya, baby. You just cry."

Ten minutes later, two patrol cars, and Nettie's pickup were coming to a gravel slinging stop in the drive. Delilah bolted from the sofa, and met Eli in the hall. Eli scooped Delilah into his arms, and kissed the uninjured side of her face, while Charlie and his two deputies holstered their weapons.

Eli pulled away from Delilah and examined her. He gently touched her cheek. His pained expression quickly turned to one of rage. "What did he do to you?"

Before she could answer, he'd turned and advanced on her assailant.

"Eli, don't!" Delilah shouted.

He stopped, and looked back at her.

"You'll kill him," she said softly.

"Well that's got my vote," Karon said as she pulled herself up from the couch and sauntered over to stand next to the deputy who was tending to Herbert. She bent over and picked up the gallon of paint.

"Look what he did to her," Eli pleaded with Charlie, pointing at Delilah.

"Look what she did to him," Charlie countered.

"What DID you do to him?" Eli asked Delilah.

Delilah's eyes went wide and she bit her lower lip. "Well, you see, I sort of shot him with the nail gun," she said innocently. "And then somehow that gallon of paint Karon's holding . . . accidently smashed into his face."

"She kinda skipped the part about introducing her knee to his Lone Ranger and the Tonto twins," Karon said pointing at Herbert's crotch.

Charlie labored to keep a straight face, while the two deputies had given up that fight and were grinning from ear to ear. Eli was marginally amused, too.

Herbert began stirring, and between groans he mumbled something like "that itch roke I jaw."

The gallon of paint 'slipped' out of Karon's hand and landed right on Herbert's head.

"Oh, I am so sorry," she said with all the compassion and sincerity of the Terminator.

"You know, Delilah," Charlie said, nodding and finally smiling. "It's a shame you can't shoot a regular pistol as well as you shoot a nail gun."

Delilah smiled, and took a deep cleansing breath. "Don't be too impressed, Charlie," she said. "I was only a few feet away from him, and it took three shots to hit him once. And I was aiming for his Lone Ranger and the Tonto Twins."

Every man in the room winced, and flinched.

"Lucky for him you're a bad shot," one of the deputies said.

As the deputies escorted a semi-coherent Herbert to the squad car, Delilah handed over Nettie's journal and the documents implicating Herbert in conspiracy and attempted murder. Herbert would have a separate charge for the murder of Murray Rockford.

"He showed up shortly after Eli left," Delilah said. "He must've been watching the place."

"No," Charlie said. "We questioned Herbert a couple days ago about Murray, and Eli. There were some inconsistencies in his statement which sent up a red flag. More than anything, he told us some things that, as their attorney, he shouldn't have told us. Then, this morning, we got a call from an old acquaintance of Nettie's from Arkansas; a Mr. Clovis. Evidently Nettie had confided part of her suspicions to him. He told us about the journal. Herbert was in our office today being questioned about the journal, when I called Eli."

"But how did Cletus know to call you?" Delilah asked.

"Gus," Charlie answered. "Evidently, he called Gus last night, checking up on you, and Gus told him everything that had been going on.

"Once Mr. Clovis told us about the journal, we wanted to find out who else knew about it. So, we asked Herbert to come in for questioning."

"Did he know?" Delilah asked.

Charlie shook his head. "Herbert was visibly shaken when he found out about it," Charlie said. "Eli, on the other hand, was not. He

WAS shocked when he learned he could possibly inherit the ranch."

"But wouldn't that have been motive for Eli?" Delilah asked.

"It would have been if,"

Eli cleared his throat, and exchanged a furtive glance with Charlie. "If other circumstances hadn't been . . . weren't in place."

"Obviously," Eli quickly interjected. "Herbert came directly here after leaving Charlie's office. After Charlie and I talked, he was convinced Herbert was behind everything. The only problem was motive."

"And we both suspected that the motive was in the journal," Charlie added. "We tried to contact Herbert again, but there wasn't an answer. Then Karon called and said Herbert was at the ranch holding Delilah at gun point. I told her to stay hidden until we got there."

"That's when she called the landline to distract Herbert," Delilah said.

"And thankfully that worked," Charlie said. "Sort of."

"We were on the way here when I tried calling your cell phone, and then the landline," Eli said. "But I guess he'd already pulled the phone out of the wall."

Delilah took a deep breath and sighed. She looked around at all the people that cared about her. Charlie, who had been so kind and honest, Karon, who was as good a friend as ever could be, and Eli. She wasn't entirely certain, but she thought Eli probably loved her in some small measure. Her brow furrowed.

"Where's Gus?" Delilah asked, suddenly concerned.

They all looked at each other. Eli pulled his cell phone out of his pocket and dialed the number at the trailer. There was no answer.

"Eli," Delilah said, slightly panicked. "If he was outside, he would have heard the sirens, and come to the house. You don't think Herbert could have . . ."

Not exactly the end.

7887968R00155

Made in the USA
San Bernardino, CA
20 January 2014